THE DRAGON IN THE SEA

DRAGON KEEPERS

BOOK 1

THE DRAGON IN THE SOCK DRAWER

BOOK 2

THE DRAGON IN THE DRIVEWAY

BOOK 3

THE DRAGON IN THE LIBRARY

BOOK 4

THE DRAGON IN THE VOLCANO

BOOK 5

THE DRAGON IN THE SEA

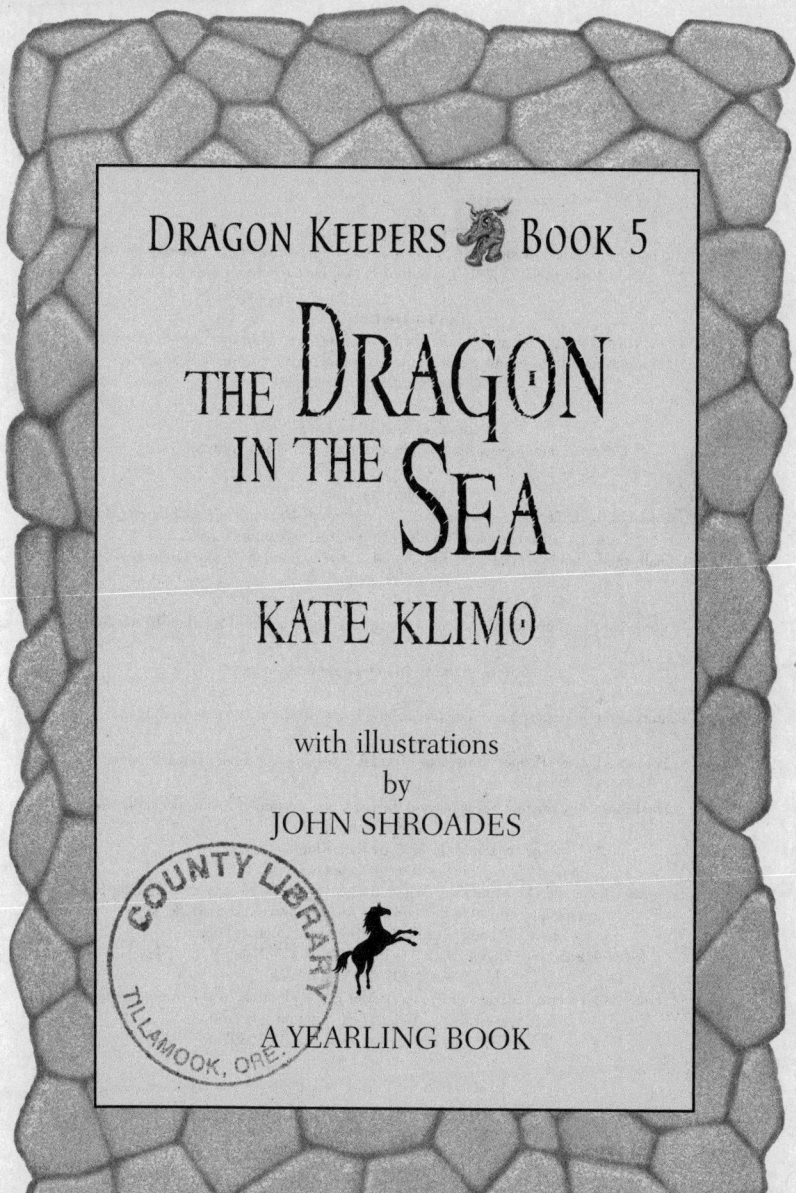

Dragon Keepers 🐲 Book 5

The Dragon
in the Sea

Kate Klimo

with illustrations
by
JOHN SHROADES

A YEARLING BOOK

For Justine,
in memory of magical Sea Cliff summers

Text copyright © 2012 by Kate Klimo
Cover art and interior illustrations copyright © 2012 by John Shroades

Visit us on the Web! randomhouse.com/kids

Educators and librarians, for a variety of teaching tools, visit us at RHTeachersLibrarians.com

For more Dragon Keepers fun, go to FoundADragon.org and thedragonkeepers.com

The Library of Congress has cataloged the hardcover edition of this work as follows:
Klimo, Kate.
The dragon in the sea / by Kate Klimo. — 1st ed.
p. cm. — (Dragon keepers ; #5)
Summary: Jesse and Daisy and their dragon friend, Emmy, try to recover a Thunder Egg
from merpeople who stole it from Daisy near the Inn of the Barking Seal,
where the cousins are visiting their grandmother Polly.
ISBN 978-0-375-87065-1 (trade) — ISBN 978-0-375-97065-8 (lib. bdg.) —
ISBN 978-0-307-97437-2 (ebook)
[1. Dragons—Fiction. 2. Eggs—Fiction. 3. Mermaids—Fiction. 4. Mermen—Fiction.
5. Magic—Fiction. 6. Cousins—Fiction.] I. Title.
PZ7.K67896Dqs 2012 [Fic]—dc23 2011030768

ISBN 978-0-375-87116-0 (pbk.)

Printed in the United States of America   10 9 8 7 6 5 4 3 2 1

First Yearling Edition 2013

Dear Reader,

I hope you enjoy reading about Jesse and Daisy's latest magical adventure with their dragon, Emmy. As you read this book, you will come across something new that looks like this: . This is a dragon footprint, otherwise known as a dragon footnote. The dragon footnote lets you know that you will find out more about the word or words it marks when you visit my wonderful new website, thedragonkeepers.com. It has maps and pictures and glossaries of characters, places, and terms. . . . In short, it's a complete guide to the wonderful, magical world of the Dragon Keepers. Please visit soon!

Yours truly,
Kate Klimo

CONTENTS

1. Zombie Fog 3
2. The Battle of the Backpack 20
3. Half-Fish 36
4. The Eighth Sea 51
5. Captain Belleweather's Cabin 69
6. The Second Egg 86
7. A Case of the Heebie-Jeebies 103
8. The Mollycoddle 117
9. A Star to Guide Them 134
10. The Wrath of the Mermage 147
11. Play Ball! 161
12. Sounding the Boatswain's Pipe 175
13. The Sacred Draconian Birthing Incantation 189
14. Golden of Leandra 202

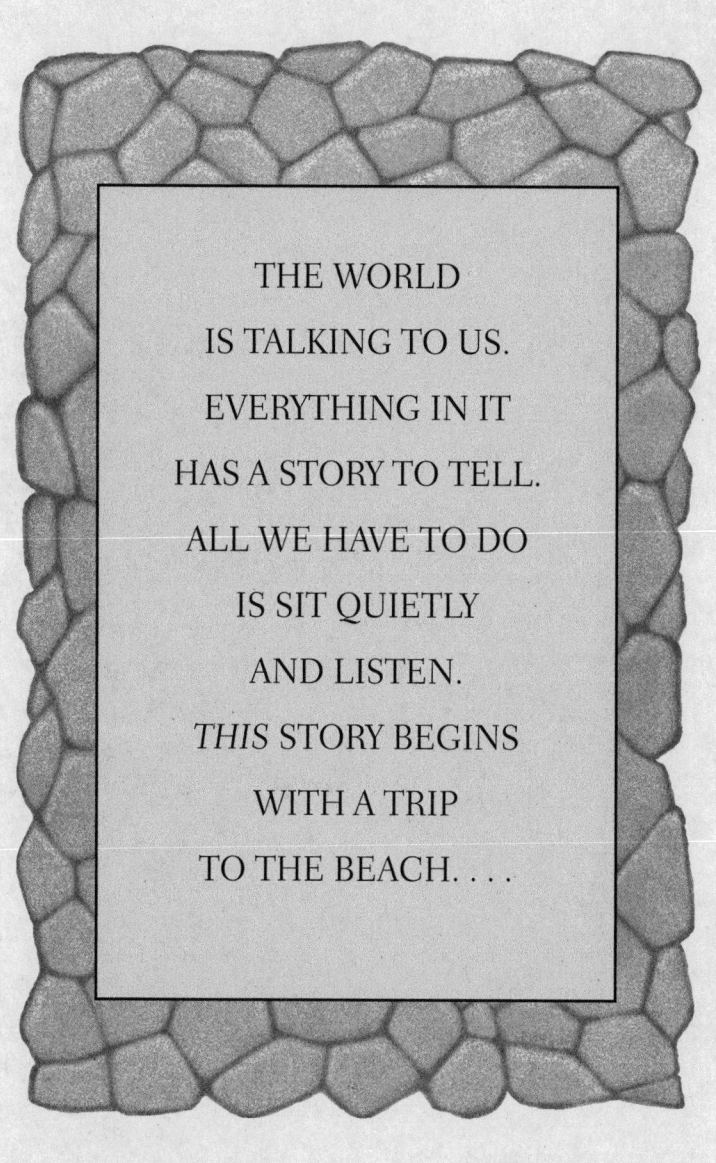

THE WORLD
IS TALKING TO US.
EVERYTHING IN IT
HAS A STORY TO TELL.
ALL WE HAVE TO DO
IS SIT QUIETLY
AND LISTEN.
THIS STORY BEGINS
WITH A TRIP
TO THE BEACH. . . .

CHAPTER ONE

ZOMBIE FOG

Dear Mom and Dad, Even though our driver got lost twice, we still made it to the Inn of the Barking Seal in time for lunch—and guess what? Those seals are still barking! There were two last-minute cancellations, so it looks like Daisy and I are going to be the only guests. What with a 26-pound turkey, we'd better make room for lots of turkey and sausage-stuffing sandwiches. Aunt Maggie and Uncle Joe are on their way to Boston to help out with the twins. This is Daisy's first time away from her parents for Thanksgiving, just like it's my first time away from you, so I guess, for once, we're both in the same boat. She is going to email them later on tonight if this computer holds out. It's practically an antique! Just in case, Mom, if you're online with Aunt Maggie, tell her Daisy misses her a boatload. And, oh, by the way, I miss you guys, too.

What Jesse *didn't* say was that he and Daisy missed Emmy right now, even more than they missed their parents. Emmy was their six-month-old dragon, who was now as big as two elephants combined. Emmy had been invited by her friends in the Fiery Realm to attend a royal runching as the guest of honor of the Grand Beacons. She was so excited, her Keepers didn't have the heart to say no.

As Jesse was thinking about this, the computer started making a crackling noise. He pressed SEND and turned the computer off before it exploded.

Then he went looking for his cousin. Finding someone in his grandmother's bed-and-breakfast was no mean feat.

A big, gray-shingled house on a cliff overlooking the Pacific Ocean, it had been built by a whaling captain in the 1860s and had since been added on to by each of its owners. It sprawled along the cliff like a train that had toppled off the track. The locomotive was the Salon, where the computer sat on a captain's desk near a sandstone fireplace. Next came the kitchen and the dining room, or the Galley and the Mess Hall, respectively, if their grandmother was giving the tour. Then, one after another, came the seven staterooms with three parlors—Red, Yellow, and Blue—tucked in here and there. Jesse came across his grandmother in the Red Parlor.

The same grandmother who regularly sent them socks in the mail, this was Aunt Maggie and Jesse's mother's mom. Jesse and Daisy weren't allowed to call her Grandma or Granny or Nana or any of the other names most kids called their grandmothers. It was "just plain Polly, thank you very much."

Daisy wanted to be just like Polly when she grew up. Polly was tall and lean, and her long gray hair was always in a braid that hung down her back like a mooring rope. She wore red wooden clogs, men's plaid shirts, and corduroy trousers. She had a way of nailing you with her sharp black eyes that made you believe she was expecting great things from you and you had better deliver. She never said typical grandmotherly things like, "My, how big you've grown," or "Give us a kiss," or "When I was a girl . . ." In fact, you never knew *what* she was going to say.

"Hey, Polly," Jesse said. "You might need to break down and buy a new computer."

Polly looked up from her crossword puzzle and grunted. "What for? I need a new computer like a flounder needs a unicycle."

Jesse laughed. "Have you seen Daisy?" he asked.

"Nope, but when you track her down, why don't you two hike to the beach and say ahoy there to the new neighbors?"

"Neighbors?" As far as Jesse knew, Polly's was the only house within miles.

"The Driftwoods," Polly said. "Bill and Mitzi. They've built a shack about six feet above the high-tide line, due south down the beach a spell. They've got kids, too, a boy and a girl about your age. Coral and Reef."

"Coral and Reef?" Jesse repeated. "They sound like hippies."

"Hippie beach bums, the best kind," said Polly, returning to her puzzle. "Only kind that could survive on *that* beach. Your cousin's probably in the Fishbowl with her nose in a book."

The Fishbowl, the caboose of the house, was where the kids slept. It had four bunk beds and overlooked the garden on the edge of the cliff. The hallway to the Fishbowl veered this way and that, went up two steps and down three, up five and down two. It listed, sometimes to the port, sometimes to the starboard. As he lurched along, Jesse passed old prints with captions like "Thar she blows!" and "Perils asea" and "Rounding the Horn of Africa."

Jesse thought Polly could open a nautical museum if she wanted to. Their grandfather, Zeke, had been "sewn into his hammock" before the cousins were born, but both Jesse and Daisy felt they knew him from his house and his stuff. A merchant seaman, Zeke had brought back treasures from his voyages around the world: Maori war clubs made from sawfish blades, Aleut harpoons, antique scrimshaw carved from the teeth of blue whales, and lots of bright work, shiny brass fittings like compasses and portholes and hinges and plaques salvaged from old vessels. There were model ships everywhere: ships in bottles, ships hanging from the overhead beams, and ships on every mantelpiece.

Daisy was standing before the mantelpiece in the Blue Parlor, her elfin ears poking through her blond hair. She was contemplating their favorite model ship. It was a square-rigger with over twenty-one miniature canvas sails and a sea serpent carved on the bowsprit. On the prow in gold-painted letters were the words *The Golden D*.

"She looks yar, doesn't she?" said Daisy.

"She sure does," said Jesse.

Yar was sailor talk for "shipshape." Polly had taught them the names of *The Golden D*'s sails by singing "The Sail Song," which she had made up to the tune of an old sea chantey. Daisy was humming it to herself now as she touched the sails, from the flying jib to the mizzen topgallant.

Jesse waited until she was finished, then asked, "You want to take a walk on the beach? Polly said we should meet the new neighbors, the Driftwoods, Bill and Mitzi and their kids, Coral and Reef."

Daisy's blue eyes lit up. "Sure," she said. "I'll get the backpack."

They stopped off in the Fishbowl to get the backpack, then ran through the garden and down the worn wooden stairs that zigzagged along the cliff to the beach. The farther down the cliff they went, the louder the *arf-arf-arf*ing of the seals grew.

On the beach, they paused to watch the waves hurl themselves wrathfully over the rocks. Even in August, this was a challenging swimming beach, but in late November, it was downright inhospitable. Slimy tendrils of kelp lay everywhere, like the tentacles of a sea monster. An enormous rock nearly as big as a beached aircraft carrier slanted toward the sea, alive with seals sunning themselves. The seals lay packed in cheek to jowl, barking nonstop.

"Why doesn't somebody throw them a fish and shut them up?" Jesse asked.

Daisy grinned. It was one of the jokes Daisy's father, Uncle Joe, never got tired of cracking. In the shadow of the seal rock, they found a large tide pool. Never able to resist a good tide pool, they knelt and dipped their hands in the clear water.

Jesse yanked his hand out. It was freezing!

Daisy was already shucking off her sneakers and socks, rolling up her jeans, and wading in. Jesse watched as she picked through the tide pool and found a few seashells. There were also some choice pieces of sea glass.

"For the Museum of Magic ?" she said,

holding up a pale green piece of sea glass for Jesse to see.

"It reminds me of the gems on the beach in the Fiery Realm," said Jesse, thinking wistfully that Emmy would be toasty warm in the Fiery Realm right now.

Daisy gasped as she dropped the treasures she had just collected. At first, Jesse thought it was because of the cold, but she was wading toward something in the center of the tide pool. It looked like the softball Jesse had lost last summer. He walked along the edge of the tide pool to get a closer look. It was definitely *not* a softball.

"Is that what I think it is?" Jesse asked Daisy, his heart starting to flutter.

Jesse charged, sneakers and socks and all, into the freezing water just as Daisy bent to pick up the object.

"It is!" she said, cradling it in her hands. It was a perfectly round rock with a rough surface the texture of congealed oatmeal. "It's a geode."

"Wow," said Jesse in a hushed voice. "A Thunder Egg . Do you think . . . ?"

Daisy looked up at him. Neither one of them wanted to say it aloud, but they were both thinking the exact same thing: *Maybe there's a baby dragon inside.*

They waded out of the tide pool. Jesse held the geode while Daisy sat on a rock and put her socks and sneakers back on. Emmy had hatched from a geode that had looked just like this one, except that Emmy's geode had had purple specks in it. This one was shot through with specks of glittering gold.

"We should tell the professor what we found," Daisy said. The professor was Lukas B. Andersson, their online dragon consultant.

"We should probably go say ahoy there to the Driftwoods first, like Polly said," Jesse murmured, his eyes never leaving the geode.

Daisy stood up. "Okay, we'll say ahoy, then go back and hop online," she said. She held out her hand for the geode. Reluctantly, Jesse gave it back to her. After all, she was the one who had spotted it first, just like he had been the one who had found Emmy's egg.

They headed down the beach, Jesse's wet sneakers making a squelching sound as he walked.

"We shouldn't get our hopes up," Daisy said.

"I know," said Jesse with a sigh. "Sometimes a rock is just a rock."

Daisy lifted the rock to her lips and whispered, "Hi there." Her eyes went wide. "Jess, I think I felt it hum!"

"Really?" Jesse said. When he had first found

Emmy's Thunder Egg on High Peak, he had felt it buzz. This was a good sign.

As they rounded the point, they saw a small, ramshackle structure made of sea salvage set into the side of the cliff. A man and a woman were digging a hole in the sand nearby. It was a chilly day but both of them were barefoot. The man wore nothing but cutoff dungarees. The woman wore a black wet suit and had long black hair that fell in ripples to her waist.

"Wow," said Jesse. "Awesome new neighbors."

"I wonder where Seashell and Kelp are?" Daisy asked.

"Coral and Reef," Jesse said with a smirk. "Maybe they're inside watching the *SpongeBob SquarePants* Thanksgiving special on TV."

"I have a feeling there's no TV in that shack," Daisy said.

"I have a feeling there's no *living room,* either. Something tells me this is not your average all-American family."

As if they had heard Jesse, Bill and Mitzi both straightened and looked down the beach, shading their eyes against the afternoon sun. Bill raised a hand and waved. Jesse and Daisy waved back.

"Ahoy there!" Jesse called out. He and Daisy walked up to the Driftwoods.

"You must be Polly's grandkids," Mitzi said. Her eyes were dark and shiny, and her voice was distant but oddly distinct, the way your voice sounds when you speak into a seashell. "I'm Mitzi." She set down a shovel made from a stick of driftwood with a large clamshell lashed to the end of it. Her hand, when she shook theirs, was as cool as an Arctic char.

The man was deeply tanned with eyes the blue of faded denim. His long brown hair was sun-streaked in ribbons of pale gold. He bobbed his head. "Bill Driftwood, groovy to meet you."

"Groovy to meet you, too," said Daisy.

Jesse could tell she was holding back laughter.

Mitzi stared at the geode in Daisy's hand. "What's that?" she asked.

Daisy put the geode behind her back just as Jesse said, "That? It's a Thun—"

"Just a geode," Daisy broke in briskly.

"For real? Did you find it around here?" Bill asked.

"We did," Jesse said. Daisy elbowed him to shut up, but Jesse was already saying, "We found it in a tide pool by the seal rock."

"How interesting!" said Mitzi, taking a step closer. "I've always wanted one. Where are the kids?" she asked Bill. "I want them both to see this."

Bill waded knee-deep into the water. He raised

his arms over his head and made a wide sweeping motion. From behind a huge rock far out in the water, two kids popped into view, both wearing black wet suits. They waved back and started paddling their surfboards toward the shore as a giant swell rose behind them.

Jesse wanted to warn them but their parents seemed perfectly calm, so instead, he said, "They actually *surf* this time of year?"

"Sure thing. Winter waves are rippin'," Bill said.

The approaching wave gathered into an enormous green-black curl. The kids stood on their boards and rode the foaming crest right onto the beach. Then they stepped off, dragged their surfboards up, and planted them, points down, in the sand. They stood next to their parents, panting, fists on hips, as if they were posing for the cover of *Sports Illustrated.* Jesse had never seen anything this cool.

"Bangin'," said Bill.

"Thanks, Dad," said the boy. "That was a gnarly set."

"Hyperfierce gnar-gnar," said Bill.

Jesse needed a dictionary to understand what they were talking about. Or was it a *riptionary*?

"Jesse and Daisy, this is Reef," said Mitzi.

Reef nodded to Jesse and Daisy.

"And our bodacious bambina, Coral," Bill said.

Coral waved as if she were wiping a pane of glass clean. Neither of the Driftwood kids looked the least bit cold. Jesse guessed it was because they wore wet suits, which made them look like seals with racing stripes, Reef's blue and Coral's yellow.

"These kids are Polly's grandchildren," Mitzi said. "And they found a Thunder Egg. Take a look."

Jesse shot a look at Mrs. Driftwood. How many people know that the ancient Native Americans called geodes Thunder Eggs?

"Radical!" said Coral. She had long black hair like her mother's, and her father's faded blue eyes. "Can I hold it?" she asked.

Daisy hesitated. "I guess."

Gently, Coral took the geode. "Don't worry," she said to Daisy with a wink.

"I am so stoked," said Reef. He took the egg from his sister and put it to his ear.

"It's not a seashell," Daisy said, holding out her hand for the egg. "It's not like you can hear the sea in it or anything like that."

Jesse directed a sidelong look at Daisy. Why was she coming off so unfriendly? Maybe she was just being protective of the Thunder Egg. But Reef didn't seem offended by Daisy's manners.

"It's all good," he said, smiling as he handed the geode back to Daisy. Reef had his mother's eyes, as shiny and round as those of a character out of some Japanese animation. "You guys are stone-cold *lucky*."

"I'd put the geode in your backpack if I were you, dear," Mitzi said to Daisy.

Daisy handed the geode to Jesse and turned around so Jesse could unzip the backpack.

"Okay!" said Jesse. Then he looked at the hole in the sand and said, "Digging for buried treasure?"

Bill said, "If only, dude. Nah, we're digging a fire pit to roast our Thanksgiving turkey. Wouldn't want to smoke up our little sugar shack."

"Have fun. It was, um, groovy meeting you," said Jesse.

"Bodacious brody," said Bill. He held out his fist to Jesse.

Jesse stared at it, then held out his own fist. Bill did a fist-bump, wiggety-waggety, chest-thump, slap-slap-snap routine that Jesse tried to keep up with. As secret handshakes went, it was just about the coolest and most complicated one he had ever done. He grinned at Bill, who grinned back.

Daisy grabbed his arm and hauled him back toward Polly's house.

"Wait!" said Mitzi.

Daisy rolled her eyes. Jesse was all too happy to spend more time with these people. They both turned around.

"Take these," Mitzi said.

"What are they?" Daisy asked.

"A little piece of the beach," Mitzi said with a smile. She was holding out two circles of fine fishing line strung through two small translucent seashells.

They were necklaces. Jesse now noticed that both Coral and Reef were wearing similar ones over their wet suits.

"Thanks," said Jesse, taking them and handing one to Daisy.

Bill offered an encouraging smile. "I always say that a piece of the beach is handy to have on you," he said.

Daisy watched Jesse put his on over his head, and then, reluctantly, did the same with hers.

"Well, good luck," said Mitzi. "You'd better run along home . . . before the fog rolls in."

Jesse squinted up at the sky. It was bright blue and the sun was shining. "Right," he said slowly. "Well, happy Thanksgiving."

"They were *awesome!*" Jesse whispered as he and Daisy made their way back down the beach toward the zigzag stairs.

"They were *weird*," Daisy said.

"Awesome," Jesse said.

"Weird," Daisy returned.

"*Weirdly awesome,*" Jesse said, settling it.

"And, meanwhile," Daisy added, "what fog?"

But no sooner had they rounded the point than a blanket of fog enveloped them that was so thick and cold and clammy, they had to grope their way along the shoreline.

"Holy moly!" said Daisy, who was walking closer to the water. "Give me your arm, Jess."

"This is some serious zombie fog," said Jesse.

Daisy drew closer to him. "Don't *say* that. You're giving me the heebie-jeebies."

Suddenly, Jesse froze in his tracks.

"Don't stop now." Daisy tugged on his arm. "The stairs are just ahead . . . I hope."

"Don't you hear it?" Jesse said.

"Hear what?" Daisy said.

"The seals," said Jesse. "They stopped barking."

In the eerie quiet, they heard the water lapping. Or was it something moving steadily toward them through the water?

Daisy screamed, her nails digging into Jesse's arm.

"What's wrong?" he shouted.

"Jess, help!" she said, her voice desperate, her eyes wide. "Something's *got* me!"

Jesse watched in horror as Daisy, arms reaching out to him, was dragged belly-down by the legs over the sand and into the sea. Jesse splashed in after her, heedless of the freezing water, as she disappeared beneath the waves. Moments later, she bobbed back up, sputtering and gasping.

Then Jesse saw what had gotten Daisy.

CHAPTER TWO

THE BATTLE OF THE BACKPACK

It looked like a giant sea horse, the color of green glass, with a black mane and a tail that curled over its back. Unlike a sea horse, it had tiny Tyrannosaurus rex–like arms that were grasping Daisy and dragging her farther out into the sea.

Daisy screamed as she went under and came up again, choking and spitting water. Jesse dived in and swam after her through the murky, churning water. No sooner had he caught up to her than a wave slapped him hard in the face. Rubbing the stinging salt from his eyes, he saw that there was a man in the water, too, who seemed to be trying to wrestle Daisy away from the sea horse.

Jesse was relieved to have a grown-up's help—until he got a better look at the man: scraggly beard, greenish skin, red-rimmed bloodshot eyes. Jesse's first thought was *Water zombie!* Then the man heaved up out of the water, and Jesse saw that, from the waist down, he had a fish's tail.

Merman! And the merman wasn't trying to rescue Daisy. He was trying to get her away from the sea horse and capture her for himself!

Jesse flew at the merman and pummeled him with his fists. When that didn't work, he tried to pry the merman's fingers loose from Daisy's arm. The merman's fingernails were long and black.

"Jess!" Daisy gasped. She flung her free arm around Jesse's neck and pulled him underwater with her. Jesse struggled back to the surface, pulling Daisy and the merman with him, just as the sea horse flicked its curly tail and came charging past him to butt the merman hard in the chest with its head. The sea horse knocked loose the merman's grip on Daisy; then it took Daisy's arm and yanked her away from Jesse. The merman rebounded and grabbed Daisy's other arm, pulling her in the opposite direction. Back and forth, the merman and the sea horse tugged Daisy. With each tug, Daisy got dunked. She sputtered and choked and whipped her head about. Jesse looked helplessly for a way to get between Daisy and her attackers, but there was too much splashing and thrashing going on. Then one enormous tug from the merman brought all three of them underwater.

Jesse dived down. The merman had seized hold of the backpack's strap and begun to work it off Daisy's shoulder. The sea horse grabbed the other strap. Just as Jesse's air gave out, he realized, *It's not Daisy they want. It's the backpack!*

He kicked up to the surface, sucked in a lungful of air, and then dived back down. Daisy had gone completely limp. It wasn't hard for Jesse to pull her free of the straps, take her arm, and swim them both away from the skirmish and back toward the surface.

Jesse felt them being lifted by a surge of current. Up, up, up they went until their heads broke the surface of the water.

Jesse inhaled deeply. Daisy's eyes were glazed

over. He wasn't sure she was even aware her head was above the water again.

"Breathe, Daise!" he shouted at her, shaking her shoulders.

Jesse had just enough time to fill his lungs with air before the wave pulled them back under, spinning them head over heels, sending them tumbling and rolling like laundry in the heavy-duty rinse cycle.

No matter how rough it got, Jesse held on to Daisy. He stuck his free hand out to break the spinning motion. Tiny pebbles dug painfully into his palm. Half crawling, half dragging Daisy up onto the shore, he felt a wave of relief when he saw her raise her head and take a deep, shuddering breath. She lifted herself up onto her knees and threw up what looked like half the Pacific Ocean.

As he patted Daisy's back, Jesse was vaguely aware that the fog had lifted, the sky was blue, and the seals were barking again.

Daisy stopped puking seawater long enough to peer up at him. "Backpack?" she croaked.

"We left it with the water zombie and the giant sea horse," Jesse said, panting. "They're probably still fighting over it. I wonder who will win? The merman was strong, but the sea horse was a pretty fierce head-butter."

"No!" Daisy shouted. She stood up and looked out to sea. "I'm going in after it."

Jesse grabbed her hand as she struggled toward the water. It sparkled in the sunlight, looking as blue and calm and inviting as a picture postcard, but Jesse knew better. That sea had almost drowned them both. "Let it go, Daisy."

Daisy's hand felt like it had been sitting in a meat locker. She was trembling all over as she crumpled onto the sand. "We lost it, Jess," she sobbed. "We lost the Thunder Egg!"

Jesse plopped down next to her, only realizing now that this was true. Daisy wept and shivered. Jesse wanted to give her a bandanna to dry her tears but the bandanna was in the backpack.

"I'm sorry about the backpack and the Thunder Egg," he said through numb lips. "But I'm *not* sorry you didn't drown."

Daisy rubbed her eyes with the backs of her hands. "I was pretty sure I was a goner," she said. "Until I saw you, and then I knew everything was going to be okay. Thanks for coming in after me. I know how much you hate cold water."

Jesse blushed. "I had to." He could tell she was feeling better, so he said, "Ready to head back up? I think we need to tell the professor what just happened."

Daisy perked up. "The professor! Of course! He'll have some ideas."

Jesse was too happy to see his cousin's spirits restored to say what he was thinking: *Only if Polly's computer is working.*

When they got back up to the house, they each took a hot shower and quickly changed into dry clothes, then met up at the captain's desk in the Salon.

Jesse switched on the computer but nothing happened. The little light was on, but the screen wouldn't come up. He tried unplugging the computer and plugging it in again. The screen remained stubbornly blank. He tried moving the mouse around and clicking it. He was ready to start pounding the keys with both fists when he heard Polly's voice.

"I have a sledgehammer you can borrow if you think it'd do the trick." She was standing in the doorway. "A little late in the year to be swimming, wouldn't you say?"

"How did you know?" Jesse asked.

"Seaweed in the shower drains," Polly said, holding up a long green tendril.

Daisy stood with her arm on Jesse's shoulder. "We fell in," she said.

Polly's eyes narrowed. "Is that so? Well now,

must have been mighty cold. Your lips are still blue."

Daisy nodded. She was chilled to the bone and light-headed, and her ears rang as if she were still underwater.

"Your computer isn't working," Jesse said to Polly.

"So it seems," Polly said. "But the fireplace is, and I think you two could use a hot fire a whole lot more than a cold computer screen. Go get some wood from the pile."

They went outside to the big stack of driftwood on the deck and returned with arms loaded.

Polly knelt on the hearth and got the fire going. She rose, dusting off her hands. "I'll be in the Galley whomping up dinner. Sit here and warm up," she said, indicating the big easy chair right next to the hearth.

Jesse and Daisy wedged themselves into the chair and watched the flames leap up the chimney. Gradually, the heat of the fire baked the chill out of their bones.

Daisy sighed. The fire reminded her of the Fiery Realm, which reminded her of Emmy and how much she missed their dragon.

Jesse sighed. "I miss her, too," he said.

Jesse and Daisy were staring drowsily into the flames when an image appeared in the fire.

It was the Fire Fairies they had met in the Fiery Realm . Spark had a head that came to an orange point like the flame on a birthday candle. Flicker flickered, white one moment and blue the next. Fiero was smaller than the other two and round.

Jesse leaned forward and whispered, "Hey, you guys! Are we glad to see you!"

Spark's head went from orange to red, Flicker flickered faster, and Fiero turned even rounder and rosier to show his pleasure.

"We need to get an urgent message to Emmy," Jesse said.

Spark nodded his pointy head.

"Tell her we need her," Jesse said. "Tell her it's an ultrasonic, super-duper emergency."

The fire roared up the chimney. When it settled back down, the Fire Fairies were gone.

"I hope they find her fast," Daisy said.

Jesse nodded.

Moments later, there was a tapping on the windowpane. Emmy stood outside on the deck. She had a white napkin the size of a tablecloth tied around her neck, and a worried look on her face. They tore outside.

"Emerald of Leandra, reporting for duty," said Emmy. "What's the ultrasonic, super-duper emergency, cousins?"

Before Jesse and Daisy could answer, Emmy's big green eyes homed in on Daisy. "What happened to you?" she said. "You look more like a seaweed than a Daisy Flower. And, Jesse, you look *messy.*"

"Daisy got dragged into the ocean by a couple of sea creatures," Jesse said. "She almost drowned. I went in after her."

"Jesse saved me," Daisy added. "Except that we had to sacrifice the backpack."

Emmy batted this away with a talon. "Daisy's more valuable than any backpack."

"Except that there was a Thunder Egg in the backpack, Em!" Daisy wailed.

"Daisy found it in a tide pool on the beach," Jesse said, patting Daisy's shoulder. "It looked just like yours, only with golden specks instead of purple, and Daisy says it hummed."

Emmy tore off her giant napkin. "Why didn't you say so? Come on, Keepers. Let's go get it back."

"It's not that easy," Jesse said.

"We need a plan," said Daisy.

"Plan?" said Emmy. "I'll tell you the plan. We dive into the sea, find the thieving suckers who took our Thunder Egg, and take it back. End of story."

"Except for, you know, the danger of *drowning*?" Jesse said in a quiet voice.

"Really?" Emmy said. "You two? You're great swimmers."

"There's a big difference between swimming in the town pool and swimming in the sea," Jesse said. "And we just felt it, big-time."

"Not Daisy Flower," said Emmy. "See? The girl has gills."

"What?" Jesse and Daisy both said.

"The cutest little set of gills I've ever seen," Emmy added.

Jesse's jaw dropped while Daisy groped her neck. Emmy was right. There were gills just below Daisy's ears on either side of her neck: three long slits.

"Ugh!" Daisy said, with a shiver of repulsion.

"Can I see?" said Jesse.

Daisy backed away from him. "Where did they come from? Why do I have them?" she said.

"They came from the salty sea," said Emmy cheerfully. "The better for you to make yourself at home there."

"Hey, no fair!" Jesse said. "I want gills. I want to be at home in the sea, too."

"What are you talking about?" Daisy said, turning on her cousin. "I'm *deformed*."

"Can I see them, pretty please?" Jesse said.

Daisy sighed. She stood stiffly, fists clenched at her sides, while Jesse lifted her hair to get a closer look.

"Wow," he said. "They're perfect."

"How can you say that?" Daisy said, pulling away. "I'm a freak."

"Well, if you're a freak," Jesse said, "then you're a stone-cold lucky freak. And I want to be a freak, too. It's magical!"

"It sure is," said Emmy. "I bet it has something to do with those cunning seashells around your necks. They've been spelled five ways from Thursday."

"*Six* ways from *Sunday,*" Jesse corrected as the cook's gong rang out.

"Chow down, or I'll throw it in the bay!" Polly hollered from the Mess Hall.

"That's Polly, calling us to dinner," Daisy said, quickly rearranging her hair to cover her gills.

"I always wanted to meet Polly," Emmy said. "How about if I—"

Jesse held up a hand. "You know the rules, Em," he said. "No revealing yourself to people."

"But Polly's not *people*. Polly's *different*," Emmy said slyly.

"Not *that* different," Daisy said.

"Whatever! You two run along," Emmy said. "I'll

forage. Who needs a delicious runching in the Fiery Realm when I can munch water rats alfresco?"

"Emmy!" Daisy scolded.

"I'm kidding!" Emmy said. "Just because you've gained gills is no reason to lose your funny bone. I'll meet you two on the edge of the cliff at daybreak."

Daisy and Jesse sat with Polly at one end of the long table that, during the summer months, was packed with guests. Polly served one of her specialties: oyster stew. Daisy usually loved Polly's oyster stew, but tonight it turned her stomach. She nibbled on the oyster crackers instead.

Polly noticed Daisy hadn't touched the stew. "I'm not offended," she said. "You probably got a bellyful of seawater this afternoon."

Daisy nodded and slid her bowl across the table for Jesse to eat.

When Polly had finished her own stew, she pushed her bowl away and sat back in her chair. "I can't quite put my finger on it, but there's something more than a little fishy going on with you two. Care to let me in on it?"

Daisy's face burned as she patted her hair to make sure it still covered her gills.

"Funny you should say that—" Jesse began. Beneath the table, Daisy kicked him hard.

"What?" he mouthed.

Daisy shook her head in what she hoped was a forbidding fashion.

"Polly will understand, Daise," Jesse said. Then he turned to their grandmother and said, "You see, ever since last spring, Daisy and I have become what's known as Dragon Keepers."

Now, your average adult would have had one of two reactions to this statement. One would have been to laugh it off as a joke. Two would have been to humor Jesse and pretend to take him seriously while chalking it up to childish fancy. But Polly had a third reaction. Polly's reaction was "I had a feeling it was something along those lines. I want to hear all about it." She made a motion with her hands, as if she were reeling Jesse in.

And that was all it took for Jesse to tell Polly every detail of their dragon adventure from the very beginning. After a bit, Daisy gave up and joined in. When they had finished, ending with their discovery of the second Thunder Egg that very morning and their immediate loss of it to the water zombie and the giant sea horse, Jesse and Daisy sat back in their chairs and looked at Polly.

Polly was silent for a long moment, a thoughtful look on her face. "Sounds like you kids had a run-in with a merman and a kelpie."

"What?" Jesse and Daisy asked at once.

"That big sea horse? It was a kelpie. They're the spirits of the kelp plants. Just like those dryads you met are the spirits of trees. I've spotted kelpies before, from the top of the cliff. They like to ride the crests of the waves. I used to see the merfolk, too, whole families of them, basking on the big rocks far out beyond the breakers. Not to mention selkies and sand witches."

"Sandwiches?" Jesse said. "As in pastrami on rye, hold the mayo?"

"Sand *witches,* young fella, as in gossipy little scuttling sand sprites who would as soon trip you headlong as look you in the eye. Folks used to mistake them for crabs, but I knew better. Haven't seen a single one of them, though, in I don't know how long. The Driftwoods, in fact, are the most interesting addition to the beach I've seen in years."

"Who exactly are they?" Daisy asked.

"*What* is more like it," Polly said. "I'm not altogether sure, which is why I sent you two down there to poke around."

"They're awesome," said Jesse.

"They're weird," said Daisy. "And Emmy said these seashells they gave us are spelled."

"I wouldn't be one bit surprised," said Polly.

Jesse and Daisy stared at their grandmother in silent amazement.

"I know what you two are thinking," Polly said, "that it's a coincidence, us all being able to see the magic side of nature, but it's not. It runs in families, and before you start thinking about your parents, I'll tell you that it usually skips a generation."

"Then I guess I can show you these." Daisy stood up and went to Polly's chair, lifting the hair from one side of her neck.

"Well, I'll be a sea monkey's uncle," Polly said. "That's as fine a set of gills as I've ever laid eyes on."

"That's what I told her," Jesse said. "But she didn't believe me. Maybe she'll listen to you and get how lucky she is."

"Emmy thinks the spelled shells gave me the gills," said Daisy.

"But then why didn't *I* get gills?" Jesse said. "I have a seashell, too."

"Well, now, that's something else to ponder," Polly said.

"I'm too tired to ponder," said Daisy with a wide, jaw-cracking yawn.

"I'm not surprised," Polly said. "You've had an exciting day. Why don't you two lubbers hit the bunks? I'll wake you early tomorrow so you can chop onions and carrots and celery for the stuffing. While we work, we'll see if we can't figure out how to track down that Thunder Egg. And maybe, just maybe, you'll introduce me to young Emerald."

After trying one more time, without success, to get the computer to work, the cousins took Polly's advice and headed to their bunks.

They lurched down the long hallway toward the Fishbowl, both of them more tired than they realized. Jesse made a quick detour into the Blue Parlor to say good night to *The Golden D*.

In the dim amber light spilling over from the hallway, *The Golden D* was eerily transformed. Jesse and Daisy approached the mantelpiece slowly. The sails of the ship model, which usually ran parallel to the hull, were now set square. And the canvas on the sails looked damp. Jesse reached up to the mainsail and touched it.

"Look." He held up his wet finger to show Daisy. He put his fingertip into his mouth. It tasted salty. Then his eye went to the name on the prow. For the first time, perhaps because the mainsail no longer covered it, Jesse saw that there was the ghost of the letters *r-a-g-o-n* after the D. *The Golden Dragon*.

Jesse whistled, pointing to the bowsprit. They had always called the figure carved there a sea serpent. Now Jesse and Daisy saw the carving for what it really was: a golden dragon!

CHAPTER THREE

HALF-FISH

Jesse woke up the next morning with his fingers entangled in the seashell necklace, but still no gills. He wondered why the charmed necklace hadn't worked for him? Was it because he, unlike Daisy, hadn't swallowed half the Pacific Ocean? Did it only work on girls? Or was there something wrong with his shell? Maybe he should go down the beach and tell the Driftwoods that his shell was defective.

Jesse lifted his head from the pillow and looked out the window of the Fishbowl to see Emmy standing on the edge of the cliff, talking to Polly. Apparently, they hadn't needed Jesse and Daisy to wake up and make formal introductions.

Their Goldmine City neighbor, Miss Alodie, was the only other grown-up, apart from Professor Andersson, who knew about Emmy. But this was different. Polly was family. Jesse hung his head over the top bunk and saw Daisy, on the bottom bunk, awake and staring out the window, too.

"What do you think they're talking about?" Daisy said.

Jesse shrugged. "The Thunder Egg. What else?"

"Let's go!" Daisy said.

They scrambled into jeans and sneakers and hooded sweatshirts and ran out to the cliff.

"Here the little lubbers are now!" Polly said. "Catch!" She tossed the cousins each something warm and fragrant and wrapped in napkins: egg and sage sausage sandwiches.

"Eat up, Keepers," Emmy said. "Once we're in the sea, those breakfast sandwiches are going to turn to mush."

Jesse stopped chewing and swallowed hard. "We're going into the sea?" he asked.

"Where'd you think?" Emmy said. "To the mall?"

"Nearest mall's fifty miles," Polly said, "thanks be to Neptune . . . *and* scarcity of population."

"Emmy was kidding," Daisy explained to Polly.

"Oh, this one's a kidder, all right. She and I are mates. Stayed up half the night in the boat shed, swappin' yarns. Emmy's stowed a super-cargo of adventure into six short months."

"You've got that right, Granny," Emmy said.

Scandalized, the cousins looked to Polly for a reaction to being called Granny, but she was gazing up fondly at Emmy. "This one's got gumption to spare," she said, patting Emmy's haunch with pride. "Well, now, since you're shipping out, I brought you something else that might come in handy." She held up a small metal tube with a sphere at the end. It looked like a miniature angel's trumpet.

Jesse had seen it hanging on the wall in the Yellow Parlor, but if Polly had ever explained what it was, he had forgotten. "What is it, again?" he asked.

"It's a boatswain's call, or pipe, spelled b-o-a-t-s-w-a-i-n but pronounced 'bosun.' A boatswain supervises the able-bodied seamen on board a merchant ship. Your grandpappy was a boatswain, and that's how he came by this pipe. This tube here is called the *gun*. It directs air to the sphere, or what's called the *buoy*. You open and close your hand over the hole to change the pitch, like this. That flat piece there is called the *keel,* which pretty much holds the whole caboodle together, and the shackle is the key ring that connects to this brass chain that you wear around your neck. Which one of you wants to wear the pipe?"

Daisy's mouth was full of breakfast sandwich, so Jesse shrugged and said, "I will."

Daisy swallowed and said, "But what's it for?"

"To pass commands to the crew when the noise of the sea drowns out the human voice. Should you happen to find yourself beset by perils, blow on it good and hard: one long burst, two short ones. Help, in some shape or form, is bound to come a-running. Now, get going before your dragon sets sail without you."

Polly held out her hands for their crumpled napkins as, with a soft *pop-pop*ping, Emmy's wings unfurled on either side of her, purple on the underside, green on top.

"Oh, well, say now!" Polly said, standing back to admire them. They weren't a bird's sort of wings, made up of feathers. They were most emphatically a dragon's sort, as intricate as a Japanese parasol.

"They're pretty enough, but are they seaworthy?"

"Don't sweat it, Granny. I'm shipshape for sure!" Emmy said as Jesse and Daisy climbed onto the narrow bridge between her wings that provided just enough space for them to perch comfortably.

"Anchors aweigh!" Polly called as Emmy swooped off the edge of the cliff and lit out over the silvery surf, the seals giving them an *arf-arf* send-off. Above the sound of the seals, they heard Polly's voice as the wind snatched it away: "I'll save you some turkey!"

The air above the water was a good ten degrees colder, and Jesse regretted not wearing his winter coat. Then, when he realized that sooner or later they were going to wind up *in* the sea rather than *over* it, that gave him something new to fret about. Daisy didn't look worried at all. Like a pale flag, her hair snapped behind her in the wind. She was grinning from ear to ear, or perhaps a more apt way to put it was *from gill to gill*.

Emmy's voice came to them on the rushing wind: "You Keepers have your seashell necklaces on?"

"Yes!" the cousins hollered back at her.

"Good," Emmy said, "'cause when I see a good spot, I'm going to head on down."

"Aye, aye!" Daisy said.

Jesse echoed this, with slightly less enthusiasm. He forced himself to look down. There was nothing below: not a fishing boat, not a seabird, not a fish fin, nothing but flat, gray water spreading out beneath them as far as he could see. Just when he was beginning to get used to the vastness of it, Emmy reared up slightly and began to head down.

"Whoa, Nelly!" Daisy shouted, her eyes wide and delighted.

"It's going to be sooooo cold!" Jesse wailed. He had just enough time to shut his mouth before they hit the surface of the water with a loud *splat*.

The impact threw Jesse and Daisy off Emmy's back. Jesse plunged into the water, headfirst. The water fizzed around him like pale green soda. It was so cold it felt almost hot. He fought his way back to the surface.

As far as he could tell, it was just him, all alone in the ice-cold sea. There was no sign of Emmy or Daisy. The shoreline was far away. He couldn't even hear the seals *arf-arf*ing from here. The inn looked like a toy train chugging along the cliff, smoke trailing from its chimney.

Suddenly, Daisy's head popped up, as sleek as a blond otter. She was grinning more widely than ever.

"Aw, come on, Jess! Don't just bob around like

a human cork! The whole point is to swim *underneath* the water. Follow me!"

Jesse was just about to tell her to give a guy a chance to get used to the water when she dived back under, flipping a graceful, silvery-scaled fish tail in his face.

"Wait for me!" he shouted, and taking a deep breath, dived under after her. He swam down, following the tip of Daisy's tail and the bubbles she left in her wake. It wasn't long before his lungs started to give out. When the natural urge to return to the surface for air became almost too strong to fight, he forced himself to continue following Daisy.

Where are my gills? Where is my tail? he wondered frantically. The next moment, he found he was leaving his own trail of fine bubbles and that his lungs had relaxed. He was breathing under the water! Exploring with his fingers, he felt them: a set of three neat slits beneath and slightly behind each ear. Could a fish tail be far behind?

Suddenly, he felt something wrap itself around his legs, binding them together. Perhaps it was one of the mermen who had attacked Daisy yesterday? But then he realized that the feeling was coming from *inside* his body. He looked down. He could just make out his legs and sneakered feet disappearing inside a silvery sheath of scales.

Jesse tested his new tail. It was twice as strong as his two legs. If he whipped his tail around, he swam in circles. But if he merely flicked the fins at the end of his tail, he banked smoothly to the right or left.

Daisy appeared before him, her hair swirling around her head like white silk. "How do you like it?" she said.

Her words came on bubbles that popped out of her mouth. There was a slight delay, like with a ship-to-shore radio. Her voice sounded a little deeper than in the air but still clear.

"This is great!" Jesse bubbled back at Daisy.

"Look at you two! You have scaly tails, just like me! Except that mine is green and yours are sparkly silver." Emmy's golden voice sounded exactly the same as it always did. And there she was, a big green dragon in the wide green sea. "This is awesome! It's just like the air, only wet and soft. And look at me!" She spun around, executing a graceful somersault. Her wings were compacted, tucked close to her body, more like fins now.

"Let me try that!" Jesse said. He tucked his tail and spun head over fins, like a wheel that was half boy, half fish.

Daisy did the same. The three of them spun around and around until they were dizzy and laughing wildly, lost in clouds of bubbles. Jesse stopped, his head reeling. When the bubbles cleared, he saw a school of little yellow fish, hovering in place, staring at them with wide, black, unblinking eyes.

"Race you to the bottom of the sea!" Emmy said, and the three of them were off.

The rays of the sun, shimmering in the water like spokes, grew gradually dimmer the deeper they swam. Jesse kept his eye on Emmy's hind paws, paddling behind her like big green fans.

Eventually, they arrived on the ocean bottom, which was covered in fine sand as pure and white as new-fallen snow. They swam about, exploring. Daisy found the hull of a rowboat. Jesse found a rusty old oil drum. And Emmy hit the jackpot, coming upon an old yellow taxicab with the checker design still on it.

"How do you think this got down here?" Emmy wondered aloud.

"Somebody must have made a wrong turn," Jesse said.

They snorted and laughed until the water was fizzy. Then Jesse swam over and peered into the oil drum. An orange claw reached out and snatched at his nose.

Jesse reared back and said, "Yowie. Do you think it's a sand witch or a crab?" He looked around. Daisy and Emmy had disappeared. His heart started hammering. Then he caught sight of them some distance off, hovering before what looked like a long, wavy black curtain. He swam toward them.

The curtain was made up of black stalks rooted in the ocean floor, their gnarled branches extending up toward the water's surface. They reminded Jesse of the Deep Woods in winter, bleak and leafless. The closer he swam, the more grim and foreboding the place felt.

"What is this stuff?" Jesse asked when he reached Daisy and Emmy.

"We're wondering the same thing." Daisy touched one of the long black trunks. She recoiled. "Ouch!" she said, holding out her hand. There were small white ridges on her fingertips. "It's sharp!"

"Must be some sort of coral," said Jesse.

"Isn't coral bright and colorful?" Daisy said doubtfully.

"Maybe it's *dead* coral," Emmy said.

"Creepy," said Jesse.

It wasn't just the dense thicket of coral that was black, but the rocks and the sand from which it sprang were black, too. The water was murky with globules of what looked like tar floating in it. The dark place extended as far and as deep as any of them could see.

"Should we check it out and see if there's some sort of a path running through it?" Jesse asked.

"I'm game," said Emmy.

"Wait!" said Daisy, putting up a hand. "Something's coming."

Jesse squinted into the murky underwater forest. "It looks like a merman. Emmy, just to be safe, maybe you should mask."

The next thing they knew, in place of Emmy was a red fish the size of a full-grown dachshund, half head with its gaping mouth jam-packed with needle-sharp fangs. The only thing familiar about her was her big green eyes.

"I get it!" said Jesse with a grin.

"Get what?" Daisy said warily. "That our beautiful dragon's turned into a vampire fish?"

"She's not a vampire fish. She's a *dragon* fish," Jesse said. "And look! She's got bioluminescence, too. See that row of lights along her body? That light could come in handy in the dark. Good thinking, Emmy."

"We'd better work out a system of communication," Daisy said. When Emmy masked as a sheepdog, one bark was "yes" and two was "no."

"I an alk," Emmy said through her fangs.

"You can talk!" Jesse said.

"Sort of," said Daisy.

"I alk ine," said Emmy.

She sounded like a kid who had just gotten braces. "Ook out!"

The merman emerged from the depths of the underwater forest. Unlike the one who had attacked Daisy yesterday, this one was beardless, a teenager with fair hair, but he had the same greenish skin and red-rimmed, bloodshot eyes.

"Eeeoooo," said Emmy.

"He looks creepy, all right," Jesse said.

"Wait, you two," Daisy said. "Be fair. Maybe not all the merpeople are muggers and rock thieves. Let's give the guy a chance."

Daisy swam to the edge of the dark area and said to the merboy, "Hi. I'm Daisy. This is my cousin Jesse and our dragon, Emmy."

"Dragon *fish*," Jesse corrected her hastily.

"Right," said Daisy. "Can you tell us what this place is?"

"The Coral Jungle," said the merboy. Something about the boy's voice was off. Even the bubbles that came out of his mouth were greenish. The merboy lazily extended a hand toward Daisy, but she pulled back.

"Hey," Jesse said to the merboy, "you didn't happen to see a rock around here anywhere, did you?" He knew how ridiculous this question sounded as soon as it came out of his mouth.

"It was about yea big," Daisy said, describing it with her hands. "It looks like a ball of oatmeal with golden specks in it."

"Um, Daise," Jesse said, "I don't think they have oatmeal down here."

"You are welcome to enter the jungle and look for your oatmeal ball," the merboy said. "Please, be our guests." He swam slowly backward, urging them to come along with him.

"Um, no, thanks! We're good!" said Daisy, hanging back.

"Maybe we'll drop by some other time," Jesse put in.

"Eee you ater," said Emmy.

The three visitors started to backstroke, slowly and steadily, putting distance between themselves and the merboy and the Coral Jungle.

The merboy called after them in his dreamy voice, "Stay and visit the Coral Jungle." But he didn't swim after them.

"Maybe he's stuck there," Jesse whispered to Daisy and Emmy.

"We can only hope," said Daisy.

"Good zombie *grief*!" Jesse cried out.

The three of them stopped swimming and looked. Suddenly, the Coral Jungle was writhing with movement. Merpeople, male and female, all of them green-faced and red-eyed, were moving forward through the brackish water, beckoning to them with their limp, greenish arms.

"Yikes!" said Jesse. "An *army* of water zombies!"

The army emerged from the Coral Jungle in a long, ragged line and began to advance slowly toward Jesse and Daisy and Emmy.

"Jesse!" they called out in their hollow voices. "Daisy! Emmy!"

"Okay, Keepers," Emmy said, rapidly changing back into her dragon form, "let's put those brand-new tails of yours to the test."

Keepers and dragon whipped around and fled. Emmy took the lead, streamlining her body and shooting through the water like a giant green torpedo. The cousins lagged behind. While they had gotten the knack of using their tails, they had no idea how to work up any speed. Meanwhile, it was as if someone had flipped a switch on the slow-moving zombies. They were going much faster and were rapidly advancing upon Jesse and Daisy, their arms reaching out, their red eyes fixed on their quarry.

"Yikes!" said Daisy. "If we could just latch on to Emmy's tail, we could hitch a ride."

"Wait up, Emmy!" Jesse called.

But Emmy, too far ahead to hear them, rocketed on into the great green yonder.

Chapter Four

THE EIGHTH SEA

The fastest water zombie reached out and grabbed the tip of Daisy's tail fin. She let out a shriek and zigzagged to shake him off, whipsawing her tail and catapulting herself through the water.

"Whip your tail like this!" she called out to Jesse, demonstrating how.

Jesse copied her and, in this way, the two of them pulled out well in front of the advancing army of zombies. They whipped along through the water like a pair of dolphins fleeing sharks.

A dark green thicket loomed in the near distance. "Let's lose them in the kelp!" Daisy shouted to Jesse.

Jesse and Daisy dived into the kelp, the slimy tendrils trailing past them. Just as quickly, they were on the other side. Daisy dared to look over her shoulder.

As if the switch had been thrown again, the zombies, now strewn with kelp, were once more moving in dreamy slow motion.

"Keep going!" Jesse called out to Daisy. "Just in case they get a second wind."

They maintained a breakneck speed until they were almost even with Emmy.

"Hold up a sec!" Daisy called out.

Jesse and Emmy came to a halt and looked back. Daisy settled on a rock near a big orange sea fan. There were strands of kelp tangled in her hair. As she forked it out with her fingers, she looked back and saw not a single water zombie in sight. "I think we might have lost them!" she said.

Emmy and Jesse swam back to join her.

"Boy, is my tail tired," Jesse said, settling on the rock next to Daisy. "That was way too close for comfort."

"Where to now?" Daisy asked.

"Beats me," Emmy said, peering around. "I forgot my undersea road map."

"I think it's called a chart," said Jesse.

"I hate to say this, guys," said Daisy, "but if the merman won the Battle of the Backpack, the egg is probably back there in that icky jungle. Don't you think?"

"Could be. But let's take a good hard look around and make absolutely sure it's not somewhere else before we go back there," Jesse said.

"Good idea," said Emmy. "But searching for the Thunder Egg down here is like looking for a needle in a smokestack."

Jesse was too distracted to correct Emmy. Besides, in a way, she was right. Being under the ocean wasn't like being on the land, where, on a clear day, you could see for miles. Poor visibility kept the undersea world from seeming too vast, but it also made it hard to figure out where you were and where you were headed, much less look for something small.

Still, it was beautiful. If the Coral Jungle

reminded Jesse of the Deep Woods in winter, where they were now reminded him of the Dell behind their house on a dew-soaked spring morning with the wildflowers all in bloom, except that the wildflowers were seaweed swaying gently in the current.

Suddenly, something small and dark came scuttling from behind a cluster of pink seaweed.

Daisy started, swiveling her tail out of its way. "What is that?"

"Sand witch," said Emmy.

"So *that's* what a sand witch looks like!" said Jesse.

"It doesn't look anything like a crab," said Daisy, peering at it.

The creature looked like a corroded knight's helmet, a dome with eyes staring out of two holes in the top.

Daisy addressed the eyes. "Excuse me, but we've lost a round rock about this big," she said, making the familiar gesture with her hands. "You didn't happen to see it, did you?"

The knight's helmet kicked up a cloud of sand and, when the water cleared, it had disappeared.

"*That* was a big help," said Daisy, lying back on the rock.

"Polly said they were terrible gossips," said Emmy. "It's probably just a matter of time before the word's out that I'm down here. Maybe I should mask again, just in case."

"Please don't!" Daisy sat up quickly. "You're much prettier as a dragon."

"*I* liked your dragon fish," said Jesse. "I thought you were awesome."

"Thank you, Jesse. And don't worry, Daisy Flower," said Emmy. "I'll only do it if I sense danger. Or need to be small."

"Thanks," said Daisy.

"Hey, what's that?" Jesse said, pointing.

From a distance, they looked like three full-grown human figures made out of clear gelatin— humanoid jellyfish with long arms that ended in silvery tassels. Three dolphins accompanied them, one swimming beside each figure.

"Underwater ghosts!" said Daisy.

The ghosts approached at a rapid clip, the dolphins keeping pace with them. What little sun had penetrated to this depth shone like prisms in the bodies of the ghosts and sparkled in their tasseled hands like Fourth of July sparklers.

"They're like rainbow people!" said Jesse.

"Actually, they're water sprites," said Emmy. "I can't remember if Polly said they were good or bad. Just in case, I think I'll mask before they get any closer." As quickly as that, Emmy was back to being a fierce-faced dragon fish.

In no time, the water sprites and the dolphins were upon them.

The sprites had no faces or features. They came right up to Jesse, Daisy, and Emmy and stopped, their gelatinous shapes shifting.

Jesse raised a hand and said, "We come in peace."

Daisy gave him a look. Jesse shrugged.

The dolphins swam up and nuzzled Jesse and Daisy beneath the chins with their bottle-shaped noses.

"That tickles," Jesse said, giggling.

"They're so sweet!" Daisy said, stroking one dolphin while another one ran its nose through her hair.

The water sprites didn't say a thing. Slowly, they began to back away, waving their tassels like an airport landing crew directing planes.

"I think they want us to follow them," said Daisy.

"Do you think we should?" Jesse asked.

"I don't know . . . the dolphins are so nice," said Daisy. She turned to Emmy. "Do you think we should?"

"Ess," Emmy said as she set off after the water sprites.

Jesse and Daisy followed through the rolling

underwater meadow. Before long, a white arch loomed ahead of them.

"It's the jawbone of some kind of whale," Jesse said. "A really big one. Maybe even a leviathan."

"What's a leviathan?" Daisy asked.

"Like in the Bible," Jesse said. "An enormous undersea monster. Look at the size of that thing!"

The closer they got, the larger the jaw became, rising up as high as a ten-story monument and lined with hundreds of sharp teeth. But it was the sight framed by the arch that really took their breath away.

It was a massive sailing ship, its hull sparkling black and its sails looking as if they had been woven of pure gold. Twenty-four sails were unfurled and full, as if in readiness for a voyage beneath the sea.

The water sprites and dolphins led Jesse and Daisy and Emmy beneath the arch and right up to the stern. There, the dolphins nosed their way up the side of the ship, followed by the sprites, who disappeared silently in a burst of bright color that faded into the watery haze.

"Now what?" said Daisy.

"Ooool," said Emmy.

"It is cool," Jesse agreed. "It's a square-rigger."

"It's got to be longer than a whole city block," Daisy said.

They swam alongside it, level with the rail, inspecting its hatches and cabins and lockers and rigging, from stern to stem, from the mizzen topgallant to the flying jib. Although she was yar—ropes coiled, rigging made fast, deck and hull spotless and scraped clean of algae and barnacles—she was, to all appearances, a ghost ship. There was no one on board.

It took them ten minutes to swim her full length, every detail somehow familiar to them, until they came to a huge striped canopy with heavy brocade curtains erected on the poop deck. It looked so utterly out of place that it brought all three of them up short.

"What is it?" Daisy asked.

"Eats me," said Emmy.

Jesse said, "It looks like something you'd see on Cleopatra's barge."

They swam closer and discovered that the canopy and curtains were not striped silk and brocade but seaweed and seashells woven tightly together.

"What's behind the curtains, I wonder?" said Daisy. Her fingers itched to draw them aside. But the others were already swimming on, so she turned tail and joined them.

Even before they got to the big golden dragon

carved into the prow, they knew what they were going to find emblazoned on the hull. Still, it gave them the shivers to see it: *The Golden Dragon.*

But they didn't get a chance to talk about it, because a voice called down to them, "Ahoy there!"

Two creatures appeared on the bridge above them. One of them looked like a broad-shouldered man wearing a black hooded wet suit with long floppy fins on his feet and hands. His head was disproportionately small and nearly neckless, and he had big, soft golden eyes and a plump upper lip bristling with stiff white whiskers. His companion looked like the head-butting sea horse they had tangled with yesterday: a kelpie.

"Request permission to come aboard," Jesse called up to them.

"Permission granted," said the kelpie in a high-pitched voice that was like a whinny.

Daisy swam up close to Jesse's face and whispered emphatically, "That might be the kelpie we tangled with yesterday. Maybe we shouldn't be so quick to go aboard."

"Yes, we should. If she has the egg," Jesse whispered, "we need to get it back."

"But what if it's a trap?" Daisy said.

"We have to risk it," Jesse said. "Besides, it's *The Golden Dragon*, Daise, our favorite ship in the whole wide world. How bad could it be?"

Daisy couldn't argue with this, so she followed Jesse and Emmy. On the way, she noticed three deep punctures in the hull. Were the three holes what had caused the huge vessel to sink?

When they reached the deck, the seal-man twitched his whiskers and drew himself to attention. Had he heels instead of fins, he might have clicked them together smartly. "Chief Mate Yar, at your service. Allow me to introduce you to Captain Fluke."

Fluke's huge eyes were silver and spherical, offering up the group's distorted reflection. Daisy was distracted by her twin reflections in Fluke's eyes, from her plume of pale hair to her silvery tail. The only aspect of her appearance that didn't please her was her hooded sweatshirt, but that couldn't be helped. A bikini top made of seashells was probably not something she could pull off anytime soon.

"I'm Jesse Tiger," said Jesse. "This is my cousin, Daisy Flower, and our, um, dragon fish, Emmy."

Yar twirled his whiskers. "Hmm, yes, I see. Don't get many dragon fish at this depth."

"Ust isiting," said Emmy through her overgrown fangs.

"Visiting? A dragon fish using words! You don't see one of those every day," Fluke said.

"She's very precocious," Jesse said, raising an eyebrow at Emmy to signal her to hold the words to a minimum.

"Lovely to meet you! We were just sitting down to sea tea. You and your talking dragon fish are more than welcome to join us," said Fluke.

The kelpie led them onto the foredeck, where a big wooden table awaited them.

Meanwhile, the formerly empty decks had begun to fill up, whether with passengers or crew it was impossible to tell. There were more seal-people and kelpies, as well as water sprites and sand witches, most of them going about their business, but some paused to stare at the new arrivals with open curiosity. Jesse wondered where they had all come from: the sea surrounding the ship or from belowdecks?

"Do pardon the gawkers. We don't get many visitors," Fluke explained.

The table was neatly set for five with a purple coral centerpiece surrounded by mismatched salvaged teacups and saucers holding coils of red seaweed.

Daisy pointed and whispered to Jesse and Emmy: "Look-it, you guys. *Tea* weed."

There were no seats or chairs at the table. Yar floated before one of the cups and pinched a bit of seaweed between his finny fingers. He nibbled at it. "Ah! An excellent harvest, Cap'n!" Yar declared to Fluke.

"Do try it," Fluke urged the others. "It's fresh, imported from the Wide Sargasso Sea."

"Isn't the Sargasso Sea thousands of miles away from here?" Jesse asked.

"Oh, nothing is very far away from *The Golden Dragon,* as we like to say," said Fluke. "Isn't that so, Yar?"

"*Rather,*" said Yar as, with crooked fin, he lifted the cup to his lips. "Well, pip-pip cheerio, and down the hatch!" He emptied the contents into his mouth. "I say! Curiously refreshing!"

Emmy buried her face in her cup and gnashed the seaweed in her fangs, shaking her head back and forth and making a fierce, snarling noise as she did it. Daisy cleared her throat and cast about in vain for a subject to distract their hosts from Emmy's ghastly table manners, but their hosts merely looked away politely.

Jesse found it hard to believe that this refined sea horse was the same creature who had head-butted the water zombie. Maybe Daisy was wrong. Maybe all kelpies looked alike.

Jesse lifted his cup and tried not to slurp. The tea weed was really good, bursting with fruity flavor, unlike anything he had ever eaten. "Not bad," he said, smacking his lips. He looked around the table and fixed his gaze on Yar. "Now, we know Fluke here is a kelpie, but what exactly are you? Not to be rude or anything."

"Not at all." Yar pulled himself up tall. "I am a selkie, at your service, don't you know?" he said.

"Selkie," said Daisy, recalling her magical myths. "Don't selkies lure humans into the sea?"

Yar chuckled. "Usually, it's selkies who come up on land when they fall in love with humans. Sorry business, that, if you ask me, living the lubber life. Anyway, I am, as I say, chief mate of this vessel. Fluke, here, is acting captain. She's been acting for so long, I daresay she's got the part." He laughed, a series of snorts that fizzed the water around his whiskers.

"Mmmmm," said Fluke as she sucked in her seaweed like a little kid with spaghetti. "Do pardon me," she said when she had finished. "I find tea by far the most savory repast of the day."

Daisy nibbled at her tea weed. "Why *acting*?" she asked.

Yar said, "Captain Belleweather, our rightful captain, disappeared from the bridge years ago when the ship went down. Haven't seen scale nor fin of our dashing captain since. Sadly, I can't say the same for Belleweather's nemesis, Maldew the Mermage."

"Well, Chief," said Fluke, "we haven't exactly *laid eyes* on him."

"Don't need to lay eyes on the villain to observe his nefarious hand at work, now, do we, Cap'n?" Yar said.

"Did you say *mermage*?" Daisy asked. "As in magician or wizard or enchanter?"

"Magician," said Yar, "of the darkest order. His followers would say magnificently dark."

"Black as an oil spill," Fluke concurred grimly.

"Is Captain Belleweather a mermage, too?" Jesse asked.

"Actually," Yar said, with a proud twirl of his whiskers, "Belleweather is one of us. A selkie, I don't mind saying."

"A selkie with formidable magical powers, Chief," Fluke pointed out. "More powerful than anything or anyone in all Eight Seas."

"Seven," said Jesse.

"It's eight, dear boy, and always has been," said Fluke.

"All right," said Jesse, bracing for a debate. "So if there are eight seas, like you say, what's this eighth one called and where is it?"

Yar and Fluke exchanged a look.

"Should I tell him, Cap'n?" Yar said to Fluke.

"Go ahead, Chief," said Fluke softly. "Tell him."

Yar turned to Jesse. "Why, I should have thought it was obvious, lad," he said. "The name of the eighth sea is . . . the Eighth Sea."

"Well, technically," put in Fluke, "it's the Watery Realm . . . but we, as its denizens, have always called it the Eighth Sea."

Yar went on. "And it happens to be the very sea in which you now find yourselves having sea tea from the Sargasso Sea with she and me. Did you hear that, Cap'n?" he said to Fluke with a rich snort. "I'm a poet!"

"Don't I know it?" Fluke said fondly. "When you've finished your sea tea, we'll take you on a tour of this grand vessel. We're quite proud."

"Justifiably, if I do say so," said Yar.

Jesse and Daisy exchanged a dubious look.

"You *do* plan on remaining on board as our guests?" Fluke said. "It's the only safe and civilized place to be in the Eighth."

"Would you excuse us a moment?" Jesse asked his hosts as he drew Daisy aside. Emmy swam up between them, giving Daisy a start. Jesse whispered to them: "Look. There's a chance the egg is on board this ship. We need to stay and search for it, right?"

"The egg has to be here," said Daisy. "Because

that's definitely the sea horse from yesterday."

"Unless the water zombie got the egg," Jesse said.

"My money's on the kelpie," Daisy said.

"Esss," Emmy agreed.

"Did you guys get enough to eat?" Jesse asked. "I don't know about you but it's coming up on time for Thanksgiving dinner and my stomach's feeling totally gypped."

"Ine oo!" said Emmy, grinding her fangs.

Conference concluded, Jesse turned back to their hosts. "We'd love a tour and we'd love to stay," he said. "But would you mind if we had seconds on the seaweed tea first?"

"How rude of us!" Fluke fussed. "We didn't even offer. But of course you're hungry from your long journey from . . . where did you say it was?"

"We didn't," said Daisy.

"Polly's h—" Jesse started to say, but Daisy cut him off.

"Polly-*nesia*!" she said brightly.

"My, my, *my*," Fluke said, shaking her mane, "you *have* swum a long way. No wonder you're hungry."

Just then, an electric eel darted past and halted next to Fluke. She reached out and touched it. The eel lit up and gave off a loud *zzzzzt*.

The door to the foredeck cabin swung open and a small, dark-tressed mermaid flitted out bearing a large blue china tureen. She glided around the table and refilled everyone's cup.

Unlike the water zombies, this mergirl did not have green skin and red eyes. She had mocha-colored skin and soft brown eyes, her fingernails as clean as ten little pearls.

Daisy also noticed that, unlike the mermaids featured in cartoons, she did not have a seashell bikini top. However, like fairy-tale mermaids, her swirling chestnut hair was all that covered her upper body. Daisy was suddenly quite happy to be wearing her hoodie.

"Thank you, Star," Fluke said.

Star bowed and swished back into the cabin.

"Star's a real gem," said Fluke with a contented sigh. "She's our mer-maid."

"We know all about mermaids," Daisy said.

Jesse said, "I think what Fluke means is that Star is a mer-*maid*. Get it?"

"Oh!" said Daisy. "A *maid*!"

"And a hardworking one she is, too," said Fluke. "She even swabs decks. It's hard to find a mer-maid these days who will swab a deck. Some think it's beneath them."

"I rather think it is, Cap'n, being in the nature

of decks," said Yar with a throaty chuckle. "Still, she is a most agreeable creature."

Daisy said, "We met up with some merfolk earlier who didn't seem very agreeable."

Yar regarded her thoughtfully. "Did you, now? Red Eyes, most likely. A shame, that. I do apologize on behalf of the Eighth."

Jesse raised an eyebrow at Daisy. If the water zombies—or the Red Eyes, as Yar called them— were the bad guys, then surely their hosts were the good guys. But Daisy looked as if she were still reserving judgment.

"Say, how about that tour?" said Yar.

Having finished their second helpings, the guests followed their hosts down to the poop deck, where the outlandish canopy still piqued their curiosity.

Emmy swam right up to the shell curtain and burrowed her head into a gap.

Jesse saw Fluke and Yar moving swiftly ahead with the tour. "No, Emmy! Not now!" he said. "We'll look later."

Suddenly, something huge and gray emerged from between the curtains and loomed over Emmy.

CHAPTER FIVE

CAPTAIN BELLEWEATHER'S CABIN

Emmy pulled back, hissing, her back fin bristling like a scalded cat.

"Hammerhead!" Jesse gasped.

Four more hammerheads followed the first, pouring out, one by one, from between the shell curtains like clowns from a car, only there was nothing funny about it.

"A whole *shiver* of hammerheads!" Jesse said shakily.

The sharks shook their broad, blunt snouts at Jesse and Daisy, their black eyes unfathomable and unblinking.

"Swim for your lives!" said Jesse.

Jesse and Daisy shot up toward the surface but the hammerheads cut them off. Two of them milled overhead and more blocked them on three sides, pinning them to the deck.

"What'll we do now?" Daisy said in a frightened voice.

Emmy let out a long, low hiss.

"I have no idea," Jesse said. "But I'm pretty sure hammerheads are man-eaters."

"Don't mind the hammers," Yar said, swimming back and dispersing the sharks with a casual wave of his fin.

The hammerheads wheeled about and disappeared back beneath the canopy.

Daisy sagged against a rope locker. Just when she was starting to trust their hosts! "Aren't they sort of dangerous to have around?" she asked.

"Intimidation is part of their job," said Yar.

"What exactly *is* their job?" Daisy asked.

"Oh," Yar said vaguely, "keeping the hooligans and the riffraff out."

"Providing some muscle," Fluke put in.

"*And* teeth," Yar said.

"And cartilage, too," said Jesse.

Daisy and Emmy nodded. Jesse, having been homeschooled by doctors, was a fund of miscellaneous information. He went on. "Sharks are cartilaginous fishes. The same material our noses are made of. A shark is like one big nose."

"Sharks, skates, rays, dolphins, squid, octopi, crabs, eels, jellyfish, and fish of all colors, shapes, and sizes," Yar said. "We welcome all and sundry aboard *The Golden Dragon*. You might say that we provide safe haven in a dangerous world."

"Haven, my fat fin," Jesse whispered to Daisy. "Those sharks are here to guard something important—you can bet on it."

"Yeah, but how do we find out without becoming shark snacks?" Daisy whispered back.

"Ater," Emmy said.

Jesse and Daisy agreed, nodding. "Later."

Yar cleared his throat. "We'll start the tour belowdecks," he said. "I think you will find it quite impressive, if we do say so ourselves."

Fluke lifted a hatch amidships and they swam down, following the rungs of a ladder nobody needed. The deeper they went, the more brightly the lights along Emmy's flanks shone, like the painted lines on a highway at night. At the bottom, there was a long, wide passageway, lit by phosphorescent seashell lanterns mounted on the bulkheads. On either side of the passageway, cabin doors extended fore and aft, seemingly into infinity.

"There must be hundreds of doors," Jesse whispered in awe.

"Depending on the day," Yar said.

"He can be most capricious," said Fluke. "One day there's a thousand doors. The next, a mere dozen."

"*He?*" said Jesse.

"Why, this vessel, of course," said Fluke. "*The Golden Dragon.*"

"Aren't all ships shes?" Jesse asked.

"Not this ship," Yar said. "Captain Belleweather made him a he and also made sure he was thoroughly magicked, from stem to stern. With the captain gone, the *Dragon*'s all we have left. Isn't that so, Acting Cap'n?"

"Too true, Chief," said Fluke.

The doors that had seemed identical at first glance turned out to be each quite different. The nearest one had bright pieces of coral inlaid to form a mosaic showing a school of yellow fish swimming through an arch of cobalt blue coral.

"Beautiful door," said Daisy.

"We call them portals, actually," Yar said. "A door is just a door, isn't it? A simple case of open and shut. But a portal, well, it's something else altogether, don't you know?"

One of Fluke's short arms reached out and grasped the white coral knob with a tiny claw. The portal swung open.

Everyone blinked.

"Ah, yes, of course," said Yar. "It's daytime Down Under."

Rays of golden sunlight shimmered through turquoise water that teemed with exotic fish, which Jesse pointed out and named from memory: unicorn fish, hawk fish, scorpion fish, parrot fish, and crab fish scuttling like spiders along the bright canyons of coral that throbbed with color—royal purple, hot pink, school-bus yellow, lime green.

"Is it real?" Daisy asked.

Yar nodded. "Oh, I should say so."

"This would be the Great Barrier Reef," said Fluke.

"That ought to do it for now, Cap'n, wouldn't you say?" said Yar wearily, rubbing his eyes with a fin. "A little of the reef goes a long way, I find."

Fluke closed the door and waited, giving her

guests a chance to adjust their vision to the much dimmer passageway.

"That was *excellent!*" said Jesse.

"Can we go back sometime?" Daisy asked.

"Certainly," said Fluke.

Daisy pulled Emmy and Jesse aside. "It would be easy to hide a Thunder Egg in one of those coral canyons, don't you think?" she whispered.

"Right," Jesse whispered back. "But would they ever be able to find it again? The Great Barrier Reef is made up of over eight hundred individual coral islands and covers about one hundred fifty thousand square miles. It would take more than Belle-weather's magic to track that egg down if they hid it in there."

Fluke and Yar were waiting for them at the next portal. If they were curious about their guests' frequent need for private conferences, they didn't betray it. This portal looked as if it had been carved out of blue ice. When Fluke opened it, they all braced themselves as a current of frigidly cold water enveloped them. It was like stepping from a hot summer's day into an overly air-conditioned grocery store. In the bright, powdery blue water, a narwhal—unicorn of the deep—poked its corkscrew tusk into the underside of a pale blue shelf of arctic ice.

"Oo old or egg," Emmy said.

"Too cold for the egg?" Daisy interpreted through shivering lips. "Then let's hope it's not in there."

"This is a portal to the North Pole," said Yar. "Close the door before we catch our deaths, Cap'n. I prefer the more tropical seas myself. Among many, we have portals to the other seven seas. No lakes, though, sorry to say. I do so like a good lake, don't you, Fluke?"

"I don't know, Chief. I've never swum in one," Fluke said.

"But in *theory*, it's delightful, don't you agree? Altogether less starchy and dense than the salt water," said Yar.

"Quite so, although I delight in the density, don't you?" said Fluke.

"That I do, Cap'n, especially because you're here," said Yar with a twinkle in his golden eyes. "We call this next portal the Armory."

This portal was made of charred wood, and it opened to Fluke's touch with a long, loud creak. They peered in and saw heaps of weapons lying on acres and acres of ocean floor.

"Doesn't look like a good place for a dragon nursery to me," Daisy whispered to Jesse.

Yar said, "This portal is my personal favorite. I've been known to while away hours here. One has only to touch a relic to relive some of the most rousing sea battles of all time: Young Caesar battling pirates in the Med, Nelson on the bounding Main, U-boats in the North Atlantic. Good show!"

Under other circumstances, Jesse would have loved to stay here and "relive" a few great sea battles. But he wasn't here for his personal amusement. Then he spied it, a pile of barnacle-covered Revolutionary War solid-shot cannonballs. It struck him that each one was the approximate size and shape of the missing Thunder Egg.

Daisy, thinking the exact same thing, had already swum through the portal and was digging through the pile of cannonballs in search of one with golden speckles.

Suddenly, her left arm started to tingle and heat up. She stopped what she was doing, shoved up her sleeve, and stared at her arm. Each of the hundreds of fine white hairs had a little tiny flame on it. It still worked, even in the water! Her Fire Arm — a war wound sustained in a battle in the Fiery Realm—only acted up when Emmy needed her or was in trouble.

Daisy looked around for Emmy. The dragon hovered in the open portal. Her red scales had faded to pinkish gray, her mouth was full of foam, and she was making a harsh hissing sound.

Daisy dropped the cannonball she was holding and swam back out of the Armory to Emmy's side, where Jesse was already tending to her.

"It must be all the iron in there," Jesse said.

Daisy said to their hosts, "Can you please shut the Armory door? Our dragon fish is highly allergic to iron."

"You don't say?" said Yar.

"I thought only dragons were allergic to iron," said Fluke.

"Well, one learns something new every day," said Yar, closing the door tightly. "So sorry, all! I trust the little duffer will make a full recovery?"

Emmy was already beginning to look better. And the flames on Daisy's arm had died down.

"Let's move on, shall we?" Fluke said.

Jesse whispered to Daisy, "They'd never be stupid enough to hide the egg in the Armory."

"You *hope*," Daisy whispered back.

The next portal was painted bright blue with a picture of a polar bear balancing on a red ball while juggling pins. It proved to be the polar bear tank of a large zoo. Through the murky, fishy-smelling water, enormous gray-white bears glided as gracefully as bulky ballerinas. Beyond a rail, they could make out the feet of the visitors, women and children and stroller wheels, gathered around the pool.

"They join us up on deck now and then, the polar bears," Fluke explained.

"We provide them with a bit of relief from always being in the public eye," Yar said. "Helps them cope with being in captivity, don't you know?"

Jesse cocked an eyebrow at Daisy. They both shook their heads, silently agreeing that this would be a very poor place to hide a dragon egg. What if the zookeeper found it while he or she was cleaning the tank?

"Ot ere," said Emmy with an impatient shake of her head.

"No, it's not here. But we have to exhaust all the possibilities," Daisy said.

"Aste of ime," Emmy said.

"It may be a waste of time," said Jesse, "but it's the best we can do."

The next portal was an ordinary gray door in an office building. The plain block letters on it spelled out LOST AND FOUND.

"Things are looking up," Jesse said, rubbing his hands together.

"Why so?" Daisy asked.

Jesse explained. "We *lost* our egg, didn't we? So we might *find* it here."

The three of them swam through the office

door after Fluke and Yar. They set about browsing the aisles of neat piles arranged according to category: life preservers from a thousand different ships and boats, wristwatches, footwear (usually singletons), toy boats, sunglasses, kites, and balls. In the last pile, Jesse spied something that looked like a Thunder Egg, but it turned out to be a soggy old softball.

"You know," Jesse said, tossing it in his hand and watching it rise and fall in slow motion, "I think this might be the one I lost last summer."

"Then by all means," said Fluke, "feel free to claim it."

Jesse tucked the softball into the pouch of his hoodie and couldn't help remembering how, when he had first found Emmy's Thunder Egg, he had slid it into the pouch of the same sweatshirt.

Fluke permitted only the briefest glimpse of the next portal, which was studded with gold and silver and precious stones. Jesse and Daisy got a fleeting impression of open treasure chests overflowing with ancient coins, jeweled crowns, and toppling piles of gold bars. The same thought ran through both Jesse's and Daisy's heads: Dragons thrived on gold and silver and precious stones. This would be the perfect hiding place.

"Buried and sunken treasure," Yar explained briefly. "This room's only for special occasions, as you might imagine."

Jesse and Daisy stared at the closed door and wondered how and when they might get a chance to conduct a thorough search of this portal.

When Jesse turned around, he was startled to find that they had come to the end of the hallway. Moments before, the hallway had seemed unending, but now it had somehow shortened itself.

"Here we are," Yar said.

They hovered before a lacquered door with a polished brass knob and a plaque upon which was etched in fancy lettering CAPTAIN BELLEWEATHER.

"Is this the captain's personal portal?" Daisy asked.

"It's the *door* to the captain's *cabin*," Fluke said. "Would you care to inspect it while we're here?"

"Ess," said Emmy emphatically.

Jesse and Daisy nodded in agreement. Perhaps the captain's cabin would tell them something about the character of its former occupant.

Yar swung open the door and stood at attention next to it. Fluke bowed and waved the three of them in. They floated over the high threshold and entered the cabin.

It was a proper captain's quarters with a big

square table strewn with charts with a brass lamp hanging over it. On top of the charts was a navigational tool, called a sextant, which Jesse recognized from the one in Polly's house. There was a high row of windows, with a porthole on either side. Standing before the windows was a long brass telescope mounted on a tripod that was bolted to the floor.

Jesse looked through the telescope and saw a rainbow of water sprites streaming past, riding dolphins. The sprites whipped their tasseled hands over their heads like rodeo cowboys swinging flaming lassos.

"Try the captain's chair on for size, why don't you?" Yar said to Jesse.

Jesse wasn't particularly interested but he didn't want to be rude. He sat in the captain's chair and gave it an obligatory swivel. "Very nice," he said politely.

Yar and Fluke watched him indulgently.

"Jolly good, what?" Yar said to Fluke.

Fluke nodded. "Now the pet," she said.

Emmy flitted over to the chair and circled above it, then settled down in the seat, fluffing her fins like a red hen.

Fluke and Yar stared at Emmy long and hard; then a knowing look passed between them.

"What's wrong?" said Daisy.

"Oh, nothing at all," said Yar. "Thought I felt a tremor is all. Underwater quakes, don't you know?"

"How about you, miss?" said Fluke to Daisy.

Daisy took her turn in the captain's chair. "I could get used to this," she said as, tail tucked neatly beneath her, she giddily swiveled around and around.

"What's the big deal with the chair?" Jesse muttered to himself as he turned back to examine the wooden counter that ran beneath the windows.

There were quills and pots of ink and a leather portfolio incised with gold lettering that spelled out the initials M.B. He stopped when he came to a large crystal sphere on a platform carved from pink coral. He tried to lift it but it seemed to be fastened to the counter. While it might be some nautical instrument he had never seen before, he was pretty sure it was a crystal ball. Suddenly, he was seized by curiosity.

Jesse looked around. Seeing the others were distracted, he rubbed his hands on the crystal the way he had seen gypsy fortune-tellers do it. In the crystal ball's cloudy depths, the Driftwood family appeared, Bill and Mitzi, with their son and daughter, Reef and Coral. They were standing around the fire on the beach in front of their ramshackle abode, toasting marshmallows. They looked up and smiled and waved at him, like a family in an old-fashioned home movie mugging for the camera.

Jesse was just about to wave back when Fluke's voice broke in upon him as he said, "Your cabin is right next door and ready for your inspection."

"Lead the way," Daisy said.

Before Jesse could show her what he had seen in the crystal ball, Daisy rose from the captain's chair with a neat flip of her fins. The others all swam out of the captain's quarters. Reluctantly, Jesse left the crystal ball and followed.

To the port side of the captain's quarters was a second lacquered cabin door with a knob of gleaming gold. The plaque on one side of the door said HERS. The plaque on the other side said HIS.

With a polite bow to each of them, Fluke said, "I trust you will find everything to your satisfaction?"

Jesse put his hand on the golden knob, opened the door, and swam inside. The cabin was divided exactly down the middle. The "His" side was done in shades of blue and the "Hers" side in sea green and deep purple. If you excluded electronic gadgets, there was everything that a boy like Jesse could ever want on his side. It was all compact and built-in, from the bunk to the table beneath the stern window where there was a wooden puzzle of a Man-o'-War jellyfish. There were trays of paints and boxes of wooden models of dolphins and flying fish and fantastic submarines and diving bells.

Above the table, a bookcase was built into the wall and contained every book that Jesse had ever read and loved, from *The Wonderful Flight to the Mushroom Planet* to the Chronicles of Narnia to *Ozma of Oz*, beautiful linen-bound editions with gold lettering on the spines. There were also books he had never heard of, with intriguing titles like *The Griffin and the Walrus* and *Norie, Nereid of the North Sea*.

The picture gallery on Daisy's side of the cabin featured prints of seashells: *Periwinkle* and *Cowry, Cup-and-Saucer* and *Angel Wings, Horn* and *Scallop*. Above a table beneath whose glass top seaweed was pressed, she, too, had a bookcase built into the bulkhead.

Jesse and Daisy were just beginning to browse the books in her collection when Fluke appeared in the open doorway. "Now, we'd like to ask that Emmy come with us," she said.

"Why?" Jesse asked.

"Where are you taking her?" Daisy asked.

"If you'll come along, I think you'll find all your questions will be answered," Yar said.

Exchanging wary looks, Jesse and Daisy, with

Emmy between them, swam out of their cabin and followed Fluke and Yar back down the passageway in the direction of the amidships hatch.

"I wonder what they have in mind?" Daisy asked in a low voice.

When Jesse didn't answer, she turned to look for him. But he was no longer at her side. What had happened to Jesse?

Chapter Six

THE SECOND EGG

Jesse, having broken away from the others, had swum back to the captain's cabin. Once there, he went right over to the crystal ball. Maybe he could communicate with the Driftwoods through the crystal ball and get some answers to his questions, like, who are Fluke and Yar? What are they up to? Where is the egg?

The Driftwoods were still standing there, smiling and waving. Then Mitzi mimed a twisting motion with both hands. Jesse took hold of the crystal ball and twisted it on its coral base. One moment he was hovering before the crystal ball and the next he was lying on the sand in front of the Driftwoods, his tail flapping in the sand. He felt a heavy, choking sensation in his lungs. He couldn't breathe!

Mitzi Driftwood bent down and said to him, in her soft, distinct voice, "See here now, Jesse Tiger. Let this be a lesson to you." She lifted her marshmallow stick and waved it over him. Sparks and molten marshmallow rained down on him, sizzling on his skin and scales.

The next thing Jesse knew, he was back in the captain's cabin. His heart was beating as if he had just sprinted a mile. When he looked in the crystal ball now, all he saw was his own pale and terrified face, staring back at him.

Jesse scooted out of Belleweather's cabin. The corridor was teeming with sea creatures, both magical and natural. There were water sprites and merpeople and selkies and kelpies, as well as all manner of fish, eels, rays, jellyfish, and dolphins, all heading toward the amidships hatch.

Jesse worked his way toward Yar and Fluke, whose heads bobbed above the crowd. When he got to them, he saw Daisy, who turned and gave him a *where have you been?* look, which Jesse met with a *wait till I tell you* look of his own.

Emmy swam up to Fluke, who said to her, "We think you'll be quite pleased with what we have to show you."

The water around Emmy turned bright green as, before everyone's eyes, the dragon fish transformed into a dragon. The walls and ceiling of the passageway zoomed outward and upward, magic expanding the space to accommodate Emmy's majestic dimensions. Sea creatures all around, including Yar and Fluke, dropped to the deck in awe.

"Thank you for revealing yourself to us," Fluke said in a humble voice.

"We were wondering when you'd see fit to do so. We are at your service, O Noble Dragon," said Yar, on one knee.

"You may rise. And, please, call me Emerald of Leandra," said Emmy in a regal tone that made Jesse and Daisy smile fondly.

The crowd rose from the deck.

"May I say on behalf of all hands that it is a supreme honor to have a genuine dragon aboard *The Dragon,*" Fluke said.

"We suspected you were a dragon from the very first moment we laid eyes on you," Yar said.

"I guess we weren't the only ones who were suspicious," Jesse whispered to Daisy.

Fluke said, "But we had to make sure it wasn't another of Maldew's tricks. For over a hundred years, we have battled over the egg. No sooner does one side get ahold of it than the other side snatches it back."

"You *are* the one," Daisy said, pointing at Fluke. "You battled the water zombie for my backpack."

"I am the one, indeed," said Fluke. "I'm sorry that you got caught in the middle of the fray. I must say, I didn't recognize you with a fish tail."

"You see, Maldew sends all sorts of dastardly spies our way," said Yar.

"I get that," Jesse spoke up, "but if you thought we might be dastardly spies, why did you give us a deluxe tour of your ship?"

"The tour is our standard method of operating," said Fluke. "You see, the tour always winds up in the cabin of Captain Belleweather."

"Specifically," said Yar, "in Captain Belleweather's trusty, fail-safe Chair of Truth."

"You mean that captain's chair . . . ?" said Jesse.

"The swiveling one you made such a big deal out of getting everyone to try?" added Daisy.

"The very same. The Chair, you see, revealed to us your true identities," said Fluke.

"We saw that, outward appearances to the contrary, you are, in fact, a couple of young lubbers," Yar said.

"Which is to say," Fluke put in gently, "a human boy and girl from the Earthly Realm."

"And, most importantly, it revealed Emmy as a dragon of most capacious dimensions," said Yar. "Which, I might add, Fluke had suspected from the very first—but did I believe her? A dragon masking as a dragon fish? A bit obvious, in my book. Meaning no offense, Emerald of Leandra," he said to Emmy.

"None taken," said Emmy. "And you can call me Emmy."

"It was your eyes that gave you away, Emmy," Fluke said. "Dragon fish don't have emerald-green eyes."

"Dragon fish generally don't use words, either, Cap'n," Yar pointed out.

"Yes, well, there was that, too," Fluke said.

"I must say, I much prefer you as you are now," said Yar. "Nasty pieces of work, dragon fish. Face full of needles and no moral compass whatsoever."

"Well," said Fluke, "now that we all know we're on the same side, shall we take our guests to see the Thunder Egg?"

"I thought you'd never ask," said Emmy. She turned to Jesse and Daisy. "Hug?"

Jesse and Daisy gave themselves over to a warm squeeze from Emmy. "I'm so excited, Keepers!" she whispered.

"We are, too," said Jesse.

"I'm just glad we came here to look for the egg instead of that icky Coral Jungle," said Daisy.

Most of the other sea creatures dispersed as Fluke and Yar led the way up to the poop deck, to the mysterious canopy shrouded in seaweed and shells.

Emmy lifted the curtain and the five hammerheads sullenly slid out. "Take a break, boys," Emmy told them.

"Do as the lady says," Yar said to the shiver.

They dealt Emmy sidelong looks as only hammerheads can; then they glided off into the deep.

Quietly but firmly, Emmy said, "I knew the egg was here all along, didn't I, Keepers?"

Jesse and Daisy nodded.

Yar twisted his whiskers. "Did you now? I'll be keelhauled if we weren't being a bit obvious ourselves," he said to Fluke.

"It was the hammerheads that gave you away," said Emmy.

"We have guards posted on it at all times," said Fluke. "The dolphin doula says hatching is imminent."

"What's a doula?" Daisy asked.

"Someone who assists in birthing," Fluke explained.

Emmy peered beneath the canopy. "I can't believe I'm finally seeing it," she whispered.

There, in the center of the enormous, seaweed-tufted bed beneath the canopy, nestled in the folds of Jesse and Daisy's missing backpack, was the Thunder Egg.

Ever so gently, Emmy climbed onto the bed and picked up the Thunder Egg. She turned it slowly in her talons. "Did my egg look like this?" she asked softly.

Jesse said, "Identical, except that this one has golden flecks and yours had purple and green ones."

Emmy sighed. "Yes, they *are* golden. Just like my mom said. Better get comfy, cousins. Do I have a story to tell you!"

"What kind of story?" Jesse asked.

"The story of this egg," said Emmy. "My mother told it to me the night we came back from our adventure in the scriptorium and found her waiting for me on the roof of the barn. She said if I ever found a geode that was speckled with gold, I must hold on to it and protect it at all costs, because it is the Thunder Egg that holds my brother or sister."

"Whoa!" said Jesse. "For real?"

"How come you didn't tell us this before?" Daisy said.

"There's a right time to tell every story. Until this moment, it hasn't been the right time," said Emmy.

"May we please listen, too?" Fluke asked shyly.

"Be my guests," said Emmy.

They all settled down on the giant seaweed bed, surrounding Emmy and the egg.

Emmy began. "Far up in the northwestern territories, two dragons lived in a cave halfway up the side of a mountain known to the locals as the Old Woman ."

"That's in our backyard," Jesse explained proudly to Fluke and Yar.

Emmy went on. "Their names were Leandra and Obsidian—my mom and dad. This was during the period the humans called the Gold Rush, when the earth shook every time some prospector looking to strike it rich blasted away another chunk of hillside.

"My parents had lived a peaceful life because their mountain was protected by the local tribes who worshiped it. They believed the mountain was the home of two fierce spirits, and of course, they were right. To keep the spirits happy, on the third night following every full moon, the people left the bodies of two freshly killed deer in a clearing near the foot of the mountain."

"Oh, yuck!" Daisy cried out.

"Sorry, Daise," Emmy said, "but it happens to be an important part of the story and I can't leave it out. What the people probably didn't know was that this was one of the few areas on Earth where the wall between the four realms—Airy, Fiery, Earthly, and Watery—was very thin. Only a powerful magic held it together, kind of like a bandage. But a totally bad man was about to come along and rip away that bandage."

"Ouch," said Daisy.

"I know who! St. George the Dragon Slayer!" Jesse said.

"You said it, Keeper!" Emmy went on. "So, anyway, one night, there was a full moon and my mom and dad were hanging out on the ledge outside their den, when some tree spirits dropped by to visit."

"Otherwise known as *dryads*," Daisy explained to the selkie and the kelpie.

"The dryads warned my parents that they were in grave danger. A golden-haired stranger had recently visited the village. He claimed to be a scholar who wanted to learn the local lore. In exchange, he offered warm blankets and seashells.

"So the tribal elders told all their stories, but only two of the stories seemed to interest the scholar. The one about how every hundred years, the heavens rain down stones said to contain the bodies of magical serpents."

"Thunder Eggs," Daisy whispered.

"That's right. And the other one was about the two fierce fire-breathing spirits who guard the treasure in the heart of the mountain. The so-called scholar had heard all he needed to hear. He said thanks, *sayonara*, have a nice life, and went away. But a little while later, a man looking an awful lot like him returned to Goldmine City, the city of the pale people. This time, he said he was president of the Great Pacific Mining Company. He laid a claim to the land, including—you guessed it—the mountain where my mom and dad lived. The dryads told my parents to beware.

"My parents thanked the trees for warning them, but they decided that, when the miners showed up to blast their mountain, my parents would just burrow deep inside and hide.

"The next day, Dad wanted to collect the monthly sacrifice. But Mom wasn't hungry. She told Dad to go ahead without her. He flew down to the clearing, picked up the two deer carcasses, and flew with them back to the cave. My mom was glad my dad was back safe and sound but she still wasn't very hungry. So my father ate both deer himself."

"Double yuck," said Daisy.

"Hey, you eat hamburgers. . . . Anyway, my dad scarfed down the deer meat, washed off the blood in the brook just outside their cave, and then went into the den to sleep next to my mom.

"'I have something to tell you, Obsidian,' my mother said. 'I have been keeping it a secret from you. I didn't want to tell you until I was sure. Obsidian, I am carrying new life inside of me. You are going to be a father.'

"But my father didn't hear a word my mother said. He was fast asleep and sawing serious trees."

"Logs," said Jesse.

"Whatever. Needless to say, my mother wasn't too happy, but she let it go. The next morning, she reached over to wake my dad. Dad didn't budge. She tried everything—jostling him, shaking him, even roaring in his ear—but he went on sleeping. It wasn't like Obsidian to sleep so late. And then, with a sinking feeling, my mother understood what was going on."

"What?" said Daisy.

"I know!" Jesse said, raising his hand.

"Shhh!" went Yar and Fluke, both caught up in Emmy's story.

Jesse said, "Someone—and we know who—slipped a sleeping potion into the deer meat!"

"Jesse Tiger, you gave it away!" Emmy protested. "But you're right. Someone slipped my old man a Donald."

"Don't you mean a Mickey?" said Daisy.

"Right! And who else could that someone be but St. George? Like most dragons, my mother knew about the healing power of herbs, so she waited until dark and then flew down to the Deep Woods to find the berries she needed to wake up my dad.

"She had just found the berries, when from up in the trees, a large net came crashing down over her head. Scary pale men with torches surrounded her. One of them, a man with long golden hair and frightening eyes, poked at her through the netting with a cane. The head of the cane was a dragon covered in crystals.

"Mom knew who she was up against, as all dragonkind know when we come face to face with our natural enemy. It was St. George the Dragon Slayer!

"My mother begged for her life. Then she made a big mistake. Hoping to soften his heart, she told him that she was expecting a baby."

"Didn't she know that St. George has no heart?" Jesse said bitterly.

"I guess you could say she was a babe in the Deep Woods. Anyway, St. George could not have been happier," said Emmy. "He had hit the jackpot: getting two dragons for the price of one. St. George put my poor mom in a cage. That night, in a nest of straw, my mother laid three eggs."

"*Three eggs?*" Jesse echoed, sitting bolt upright.

"Three eggs. That's what she told me and she ought to know," said Emmy. "Meanwhile, back on the mountain, my father woke up from his long sleep with one ultra-supersonic doozy of a head- ache. He couldn't find my mother anywhere. Out- side the cave, the dryads were waiting for him with more bad news. They had witnessed what had gone down in the Deep Woods, and they told him that my mother was being held captive in a cage.

"The next part is too sad to tell, but, trust me, my dad fell asleep that night, after crying a brook."

"I think it's a river," said Jesse.

"An ocean is probably more like it," Daisy said. "Poor Obsidian!"

"It was the first time the two of them had ever been apart and my father took it hard. That night, Obsidian had a dream. In his dream, the Old Woman herself, Mother of the Mountain, came to him. She gave him the recipe for a spell that would help him save Leandra. The Old Woman said, 'Once you cast the spell, know that only a magic greater than it, and either of you, will be able to reverse it.'

"When he woke up, my father gathered the ingredients for the spell. He made a fire and tossed the ingredients into it, one by one. The fire crackled and popped and shot out a bolt of lightning that lifted my dad high into the air and then smashed him against the side of the mountain. He was knocked out cold. Again.

"My poor old dad woke up the next morning with an even worse headache than the one he had the day before and a humungous thirst. He staggered to the brook and leaned over to dip his snout into the water. The sight of his reflection in the water blew him away. This was no dragon staring back at him. This was a man with broad shoulders, dark silvery hair, and black eyes."

"Whoa!" said Jesse. "You mean the spell turned your father into a human being?"

"That's right, Jesse Tiger. He was looking at pink skin instead of silver scales, fingers instead of talons, and what had happened to his long beautiful tail? No offense, but he was totally bummed. He fell to his knees and sobbed his brand-new human heart out.

"But the Mother of the Mountain came to him again. She said, 'Don't fret. In your man form, you will be better able to rescue Leandra.'

"So Obsidian got a grip and dunked his head into the icy-cold brook."

Emmy sighed and settled into silence.

"Then what happened?" Daisy asked.

"Well," Emmy said, "then my dad sneaked through the woods, found the cage, and unlocked it. When he saw the eggs, he fell to his knees and wept. At first, my mom didn't understand who this man was who was kneeling before the nest of eggs, weeping. When he told her that he was Obsidian, she didn't believe him at first. Then he told her about the Old Mother giving him the ingredients for the spell that would turn him into a human so he could rescue her. And when he told her that only a magic greater than it, and either of them, would be able to reverse the magic and turn him back into a dragon, it was my mother's turn to cry. Would their babies ever see the handsome dragon that had once been Obsidian? They were both sobbing fit to bust when St. George jumped out of the bushes.

"All at once, the woods were crawling with miners armed with rifles and pickaxes. 'Save the eggs!' my mother told my father, giving him two of the three. She told him in a rush, 'Hide one in the eagles' aerie on our mountain and the other in our brook.' She took charge of the third egg—which was me. My father ran off, leaving my mother to fend for herself."

"That wasn't very nice!" Jesse protested.

Emmy shrugged. "But sensible. In his human form, my dad was no match for a big-time bad guy like St. George.

"My mother took my egg and flew to the slopes of High Peak, where she hid it, moments before St. George hunted her down and slew her," Emmy said.

Jesse and Daisy both sighed.

Then Daisy asked, "And your father?"

"He did what my mom asked him to do. I'm guessing, since this egg wound up in the sea, that this is the one he hid in the brook."

They all stared at the Thunder Egg in a kind of mute wonderment.

Daisy broke the silence. "I don't get it. How did the egg get all the way from the brook to the sea?"

"It's just like Uncle Joe says," Jesse answered. "Everything on Earth is connected to everything else: the brook runs into a stream, the stream runs into a river, the river runs down to the ocean."

"According to Watery Realm legend," Yar said, "the egg was first found at the turn of the old century on a sandbar near the mouth of the Rushing River."

"There you go," said Emmy.

"Okay, then what happened to your dad?" Daisy asked.

"Now *that*," said Emmy with a crafty gleam in her eye, "is a story for another time."

Just then, as if the tiny dragon inside had been listening to every word of the story, the Thunder Egg started, ever so faintly, to vibrate.

Chapter Seven

A CASE OF THE HEEBIE-JEEBIES

While Emmy had been telling her story, the water outside the canopy had been turning a deeper, darker green.

"Who knew there was nighttime under the sea?" Daisy said.

"The same sun rises and sets over the sea," Jesse said sleepily, "and it has set, for sure."

"I'm pooped!" said Daisy.

"Well, it's a good thing you're on the poop deck, then, isn't it, Daisy?" said Emmy with a chuckle.

"I'm too tired to laugh," Jesse said. "Even my tail is tuckered out. In fact, I don't think I have the strength to swim down to our cabin. Emmy, can't I just curl up and sleep here with you and the egg?"

"Me too," said Daisy. "We want to be here when the egg hatches."

"It won't hatch tonight," said Emmy.

"How come you're so sure?" Daisy asked.

It was Jesse who answered. "About twenty-four hours after Emmy's egg started vibrating, it went *ka-blam*. So it will probably be the same with this one. Right, Em?"

Emmy replied with an openmouthed yawn, showing the bright pink inside of her mouth and unfurling her long, forked tongue.

The hammerhead shiver swam back into view.

"Will you be okay here without us?" Daisy asked Emmy, casting a wary look at the hammerheads.

"Don't worry, Daise," Emmy said. "They're more scared of me than I am of them. Besides, we're all here to protect the egg."

"You needn't worry yourselves," said Fluke. "Yar and I will be here, too, keeping a vigilant watch."

"Get ourselves a little practice being Keepers, eh what?" Yar said.

"Quite." Fluke tapped a passing eel, and the loud *zzzzt* sound once again summoned Star the mer-maid. "Escort our guests to their cabin, will you, dear?" said Fluke.

"Yes, ma'am," Star replied with a graceful little dip.

Jesse thought he detected a particularly sharp gleam in her eye.

Star waited while Daisy and Jesse gave Emmy a big hug.

"Sure you'll be okay?" Daisy asked. She looked out into the surrounding waters, expecting an army of water zombies to be amassing. But she saw the more comforting sight of water sprites mounted on dolphins, circling the ship, their tasseled hands held aloft like the torches of night watchmen.

"Right as right can be," said Emmy, gazing tenderly down upon the egg. "We'll both be fine."

Jesse leaned over and pressed his lips lightly to its bumpy surface. "Good night, sleep tight, don't let the sea fleas bite." He looked up at Daisy and Emmy. "The egg stopped vibrating. Do you think it's asleep?"

"Wee thing's got the right idea, in my humble opinion," said Yar.

Holding an illuminated conch shell aloft, Star led the way toward the amidships hatch.

"Do you think Fluke and Yar will be the new dragon's Keepers?" Daisy asked.

"Ra*ther*," said Jesse, twisting an imaginary set of whiskers and giving a Yarish *snort-snort*.

Daisy giggled, then said, "Seriously?"

"I don't know," said Jesse. He gave Daisy a searching look. "You aren't actually thinking that *we'd* be its Keepers, are you?"

"Well . . . ," Daisy said, drawing the word out as they swam after Star down the hatch. It was like descending into a deep, dark well. "Actually, I kind of, sort of, really was thinking that."

"Really?" Jesse said.

"Well, I did find the egg," Daisy said.

"No offense, Daise, but it seems like everybody and his uncle has found this egg at least once over the past century," Jesse said.

"What you say is true," said Star, pausing ahead of them. "My mother found it once. And I had a cousin who came across it when she was playing horseshoe crab croquet in Half Moon Bay."

"But I was the one who found it this close to hatching," Daisy said. "And think of it, Jesse. Remember how cute Emmy was when she was a teeny-tiny little thing?"

"She was adorable," Jesse said. He remembered being in the kitchen trying desperately to find something to feed the demanding newborn dragon. He had had to wear one of Daisy's purple kneesocks on his hand to protect himself from Emmy's needle-sharp talons. "She was also a handful."

"But it would be different now. We're experienced Keepers. Besides, Emmy could help us. And wouldn't it be nice for Emmy to be a big sister?" Daisy said in a dreamy voice.

"She'll be a big sister whether we're the Keepers or not," Jesse pointed out. "And, honestly? I think Emmy's all the dragon we need."

"You're probably right," Daisy said, heaving a bubbly sigh.

They were swimming down the lower hallway, which was much brighter than above deck. In addition to the glowing seashell sconces on the bulkheads, the portals were lined with electric eels, blinking as brightly as the neon lights in Times Square.

"Does this place stay open all night?" Jesse asked Star.

"Night is the best time to cruise the portals," Star said.

Jesse and Daisy looked down the long, endless hallway and saw merfolk and water sprites, kelpies and selkies darting in and out of doors.

"It's something to do when you're stuck on board this tub," Star said.

"What's your favorite portal?" Daisy asked the mer-maid.

Star spun around and swam up close to Jesse and Daisy. "None of them," she confessed in a whisper. "It's the Earthly Realm that flitters *my* fins."

"Really?" said Jesse.

Star brought her face up close to Jesse's and Daisy's. "Don't tell Fluke and Yar—they think it's dangerous to leave the vessel—but I go out all the time . . . when I'm off duty, mind you."

"You go out? Really? Where?" Jesse asked.

"I go up top," she said with an impish twinkle in her eye.

"Up top?" Jesse and Daisy echoed.

"You know. To the surface, where you're from," she said. "I've even made friends with a boy and girl. We ride the surf together. They do it on boards but I just use my tail. It's totally radical and gnarly, dude!"

Jesse and Daisy shared a look of surprise. "Reef and Coral!" they exclaimed.

"You know my boy and girl?" Star asked. "Oh, I do think they are the nicest children anyone ever could meet. I get sad when their parents call them in. I would so love to follow them up onto the beach, but without legs, I can't. Tell me," she asked wistfully, "what's it like to have legs? Is it better than having a tail?"

Jesse thought of how it felt to run and jump and kick his heels. He thought of his one full day with a fish's tail. Legs or tails? A tail was great but it narrowed your options. When you had legs, you could be on the land *and* swim in the water. With a tail you were stuck forever in the water. He remembered how helpless he had felt on the beach in front of the Driftwoods' shack this afternoon and suddenly found himself feeling a little sorry for Star. So he shrugged and said, "Legs are okay, I guess. But tails are more fun."

"Really?" she said, narrowing her eyes. "Or are you just saying that to make me feel better?"

"Really!" Daisy said, clasping Star's hand. "I've never had so much fun as I've had today, swimming around with this tail. It's beautiful under the sea. Weightless and free. I *love* it!"

The portals had dwindled down to plain lacquered doors. It was darker, too, and Star had to use the conch lantern to light the way.

Jesse asked, "What makes that shell light up like that?"

Star stopped and turned, the lantern shedding a golden halo of light in the dark passageway. "It's the phosphairies. See?" She held out the shell.

Jesse and Daisy peered inside. A ring of glowing miniature merfolk with tails and finny wings swam in a bright circle inside.

"Nifty," said Jesse. "I mean, gnarly."

When they arrived at their cabin, they found two conch shells lying on either side of the door. Star bent down and shook some of the phosphairies into them, handing one each to Jesse and Daisy.

"Brekkie is at six bells. Sleep well," said Star as she swam off down the corridor.

"Wake me up if I sleep through brekkie bells," Jesse mumbled to Daisy as they swam into their cabin.

"I like Star," said Daisy.

"I like her, too," said Jesse. "And she likes Reef and Coral. After what happened this afternoon, I wasn't so sure about their mom, but I'm thinking maybe my first impression was right about her, too."

"Jess, what in Sam Hill are you *talking* about?" Daisy asked.

Jesse removed from his sweatshirt pouch the softball he had picked up in the Lost and Found and placed it next to his phosphairy lantern on the bunk-side table. "You know how you didn't much like the Driftwoods when we first met them? Well, I saw them again today, and I tell you, the mother acted like a *witch*," he said, pulling up his seaweed blanket and yawning. "But now I'm thinking maybe she isn't so bad, after all. Maybe she was trying to tell me something. How do you make this lantern go out?"

Daisy said, "Try blowing on it. What's this about seeing the Driftwoods, Jess? I didn't see them. Tell me what's going on."

Jesse blew lightly on his conch shell, and sure enough, the phosphairies extinguished their light. He lay back and closed his eyes. "I'll tell you about it tomorrow. I'm too tired to talk right now. I need to . . ." And just like that, Jesse fell fast asleep.

Daisy was tired, too, but Jesse had gotten her mind churning with all his mysterious talk about the Driftwoods. On top of Emmy's story, it was enough to keep a person awake all night. She would have to read herself to sleep. She chose a book from her bookcase, then slid under her own seaweed quilt and started reading.

It was a story about a human girl who went out in a rowboat to fish one day and got lost in the fog. When the fog lifted, she found herself in a sea of beautiful giant flowers. She had just met a little mergirl her own age who made her home in one of the big bell-shaped blossoms, when Daisy drifted off to sleep.

Daisy awoke suddenly in the deepest darkness she had experienced since being trapped in the mines of the hobgoblins. The lantern was dark but she didn't remember blowing it out. At first, the darkness was alarming. Then she breathed deeply and told herself, *I'll turn over in my bunk and go back to sleep until six bells.* She was just drifting off again when she heard the noise.

It was a steady *squeak-squeak*ing sound.

She sat up and cocked her ear. It was the sound of something rubbing against glass and it was giving her a serious case of the heebie-jeebies.

Daisy slithered out of her bunk and swam over to the row of windows set high on the wall. An eerie yellow light shone from somewhere outside. Suddenly, a greenish face pressed itself against the glass. Daisy pulled back with a gasp. It was a mermaid with red-rimmed, bloodshot eyes. She scraped at the glass with long, blackened fingernails—*squeak! squeak!*—as if begging to be let in.

In a flash, Daisy was over at Jesse's bunk, shaking him awake.

"What? What?" he said, his voice making pale,

sparkling bubbles in the dark water. "I was just resting."

He sat up and shook his phosphairy lantern until it lit up, as Daisy pulled him over to the window.

"What?" said Jesse, staring through the glass.

The face was no longer there.

Daisy tapped the glass with her fist. "It was a water zombie, Jess. A girl one. She was right there a minute ago. I saw her, I swear!" Daisy said.

"I believe you," Jesse said. Then he did what his mother always had done when he was little and shadows outside his window gave him the heebie-jeebies. He took the extra blanket off his bed and draped it over the windows. "Better?" he asked.

Daisy nodded, but Jesse could tell she was still spooked.

"We could go up to the poop deck and report it to Yar and Fluke," he suggested.

Daisy thought about the long corridor full of portals and the hatchway that was like a deep, dark well. "No," she said. "I'm sure the hammerhead shiver will protect us."

Jesse nodded. He swam back to his bunk, and that was when he saw it—or rather, *didn't* see it.

"My softball. Somebody took it, Daisy," he said in a quiet voice. "I put it on the table right here next to the lantern . . . and now it's gone."

"Are you sure?" Daisy had snuggled back under the covers. "Check under the bunk. Maybe it rolled away."

Jesse swam around with his lantern and checked, but the softball was not anywhere in the cabin. Now Daisy was asleep and Jesse lay wide-awake. He wondered who would have taken his softball, and *why*?

Jesse woke Daisy up the next morning, hovering beside her bunk, holding a chipped soup bowl. The seaweed inside the bowl looked like dark blue shredded wheat.

Daisy sat up and Jesse handed her the bowl.

"Brekkie in bed," he said.

"Don't you mean *bunk*?" Daisy said as she sat up. "How is everything going in the deep blue sea?"

Jesse pointed to the windows. Through the sun-shot water, a shiver of hammerhead sharks swam by.

"I never thought I'd be happy to see sharks," said Daisy.

"Eat up," Jesse said. "When you're finished with your brekkie, we're expected down the hall in the Buried Pirate Treasure Portal for the mollycoddle."

"What's a mollycoddle?" Daisy asked around a mouthful of seaweed that tasted much better than it looked.

"I have no idea but it must be a big deal. Hundreds of selkies and kelpies and sprites and merfolk are pouring in there."

"How long have you been awake?" Daisy asked.

"I was hungry. I went up and had early brekkie with the cap'n and the chief and Emmy."

"And the egg?" Daisy asked.

"The egg didn't have breakfast but Emmy ate with one hand and held the egg with the other. She said it's starting to heat up."

"That means it will hatch soon for sure!" Daisy said, setting her bowl down on the table by her bunk. Sweeping aside the covers, she tumbled headfirst out of the bed. "I forgot for a minute I didn't have legs."

"The exact same thing happened to me," said Jesse.

Just then, Star darted into the cabin. She had piled her long dark hair on top of her head and wrapped it in strings of pink pearls.

"You look so pretty!" Daisy said.

"Thank you, miss. Would you like me to dress your hair?" Star offered.

"Would you, please?" Daisy asked. She had never had her hair dressed before. "And what's a mollycoddle?"

"You'll see," said Star with a mysterious gleam in her eyes. She ran a small mother-of-pearl comb through Daisy's hair until it was as smooth as corn silk. Then, with a quick twist, she bound it on top of Daisy's head and held it in place with the comb.

"Thank you!" said Daisy, looking at her blurred reflection in a silver hand mirror. She thought she made a pretty respectable mermaid. Then she stuck out her tongue and crossed her eyes.

"If you ladies are ready," Jesse said, "I'd really like to get to the mollycoddle."

Star led Jesse and Daisy down the corridor, which today had totally different portals. They finally came to the gold and silver and gem-studded door Yar had shown them the day before.

"Get ready for the mollycoddle," Star said as she opened the portal and hovered to one side.

Chapter Eight

THE MOLLYCODDLE

Inside the portal, it looked like the Sultan of Baghdad himself was throwing a wild party in Aladdin's cave. Everywhere Daisy and Jesse looked, treasure chests overflowed with precious gems and jewels, and barrels brimmed with gold and silver coins.

"Wow!" said Jesse. "It's like all the sunken treasure in the whole wide world is right here."

"That's most astute, young man," said Yar, swimming up to them. He wore a heavy necklace with a rampant lion on it. "I see you admiring my gewgaw here. Fiendishly decorative stuff, which is why we hold all of our fetes here—aquinalias, sprees, cavorts . . . mollycoddles, in particular. And if I do say, this is the mollycoddle to end them all. No one in the Eighth would dream of missing it."

"What *is* a mollycoddle?" Daisy asked.

Jesse broke in. "I don't want to spoil the mollycoddle or anything, but Daisy saw a water zombie at our cabin window last night."

"A what?" Yar said, cocking a budlike ear toward Jesse.

"You know, a mermaid with green skin and red-rimmed bloodshot eyes," Jesse said.

"Ah! A Red Eyes. Did you now?" Yar asked. "A sign of their desperation, no doubt. They seldom stray far from the Coral Jungle. Not to worry, my dear," he said to Daisy. "Security on board this ship has never been tighter in general, and in this portal in particular."

It was at that point that they happened to notice the shivers of sharks of all kinds—great whites, hammerheads, threshers—cruising the portal.

In light of all this muscle (and cartilage), Jesse felt foolish bringing up his lost softball, so he kept it to himself. There certainly was a lot to take his mind off the loss.

"We know that shark groups are called shivers. I wonder what they call a group of merpeople?" Daisy wondered aloud.

Jesse turned to Yar. "Do you know?" he asked.

Yar stroked his whiskers thoughtfully. "Why, I do believe that a group of merfolk is called a *welter* . . . unless they are all of the female persuasion, and then it's called a *bevy*. A male group is called a *heft*."

"And a group of selkies?" Jesse asked.

"A group of us selkies is a *tide* . . . and, just in case you're curious, it's a *drift* of kelpies, don't you know?" Yar said.

There was a massive welter of merfolk here, from gray-bearded grandfathers down to toddlers and tiny little babes in their mothers' arms. There were tides of selkies of all shapes and sizes and drifts of kelpies—and every single one of these creatures, young and old, was draped in precious jewels.

"Do feel free to deck yourselves out!" Yar said.

"There's plenty to go around. Of course, it's understood that nothing leaves the portal. I've posted a couple of bull sharks at the entrance just to make sure no slippery customers make off with the goods, don't you know?"

"Hey, Keepers!" Emmy called out. She stood beside an enormous, open abalone shell, its top draped with strings of pearls and emeralds and rubies and sapphires. The bottom of the shell was filled with fine white sand, and in its center, the Thunder Egg lay nestled in the backpack.

"Aw," said Jesse, "it's like an undersea whatchamacallit. One of those baby basket thingies."

"A *bassinet*!" said Daisy. "That's it! I know what a mollycoddle is, Jess! A mollycoddle is a baby shower!" Daisy exclaimed happily.

"Oh!" said Jesse. "Of course! And Emmy's kind of sitting in for her mother."

Seeing Emmy in her jaunty crown of topaz was enough to get Jesse and Daisy in the party spirit. Jesse found a simple golden crown with rubies and an armband big enough to fit around his hoodie sleeve. Daisy, not wanting to mess up her hair, settled on a necklace of emeralds and a ring with a diamond the size of a pigeon's egg.

Fluke swam to the center of the gathering and clapped her tiny hands together. For tiny

hands they produced surprisingly loud claps.

Everyone stopped swimming and talking and bubbling and turned his or her attention to Fluke.

"As acting captain of *The Golden Dragon*, I am chuffed to report that, once again, the precious Thunder Egg is in our possession," Fluke announced.

"Who's got the egg now, eh?" Yar shouted.

The crowd shouted back, "WE'VE GOT THE EGG!"

"It's like a cross between a baby shower and a pep rally," Jesse whispered to Daisy.

"I am even happier to report that, after all these many long years, our little dragon will soon hatch," said Fluke.

The water filled with a joyous burbling until a dip of Fluke's nose brought on quiet and stillness again. "Present for the hatching, I am pleased to say, is the hatchling's own sister, the honorable Emerald of Leandra and her Keepers, the Venerable Daisy Flower and Jesse Tiger."

"Venerable?" Daisy muttered to Jesse. "Is that good?"

"I hope so," Jesse muttered back.

"Without further ado, let the coddling commence!" Fluke shouted. Fluke swam over to hover next to Yar, who stood, fins planted in the sand on

one side of the abalone shell while Emmy stood on the other. Jesse and Daisy settled in next to Yar.

A long line of blue crabs ran their claws across fish line stretched taut over clamshells.

"Sounds sort of like the Peking Opera," Jesse said to Daisy.

Daisy had never heard Chinese opera before but she liked this music. It sounded like Munchkins humming. As the music played, a procession of guests came before the shell and laid their gifts in the soft white sand before the guest of honor: the Thunder Egg.

Daisy clamped her hand around Jesse's arm. "But, Jesse, this is terrible!"

"What's terrible, Daise?" he asked.

"We don't have a present!" she said.

"I'm sure our presence is all the present the little guy needs," said Jesse. "Besides, we've brought the best present of all: Emmy!"

"That's true," said Daisy thoughtfully.

An ebony-skinned mermaid with long braids swam up carrying a basket overflowing with starfish.

"Starfish?" Jesse said. "Weird gift."

"Ah, but watch and see, my boy," said Yar.

The mermaid dumped the starfish out in the sand before the shell bassinet and the starfish leapt

up and formed themselves into a big ball. Then the ball collapsed and the starfish piled into an elaborate tower. The tower toppled and rematerialized into an elegant sailing ship.

"I get it!" said Jesse. "They're kind of like rubbery, self-assembling LEGOs."

"The baby will like it, don't you think?" Yar said.

"I don't know about the baby," Jesse said, "but *I* sure do."

A gray selkie with brown spots stepped up next and bowed low before the bassinet, then held up a large sea anemone. The anemone glowed like a blue pumpkin.

At the selkie's invitation, Fluke peered down into the hole in the top of the anemone. "Oh, how lovely!" she said, then beckoned to Jesse and Daisy. The cousins swam over and looked down into the center of the anemone. Inside, blue and orange and golden lights rippled and danced.

"A fragment of the aurora borealis," Fluke explained, "captured from far up north. It will make a soothing light for the babe."

"A northern lights night-light! Wow!" Jesse said to Daisy. "This kid's getting a lot of neat presents."

Daisy nodded.

Jesse thought back to Emmy's birth. Emmy hadn't received a single present. All she had gotten was a purple kneesock that doubled as a blanket and a scarf.

A small kelpie followed the selkie, holding what looked like a big clear plastic ball.

"It's a beach ball, don't you know?" said Yar, taking it from the kelpie and showing it to Jesse and Daisy.

"How nice," Daisy said politely.

Yar shook the beach ball, and water sloshed and foamed inside. Suddenly, a lifelike picture formed inside the ball of waves crashing against a jagged coastline. "This would be Big Sur," Yar said. "Go ahead, shake it and see what you get." He handed the ball to Jesse.

Jesse shook the ball and the miniature Big Sur scene gave way to swaying palm trees on a white sandy beach and minute surfers riding a giant curl. "That's the pipeline at Oahu," he said. Then Jesse shook the ball again and saw high stone walls reflected in still green waters. "That's either Norwegian fjords or the coast of Chile. Get it, Daise? It's not a beach ball, it's a *beach* ball: the ball shows you all different beaches and shorelines from around the world."

"Cool," said Daisy, taking the ball and shaking up more beaches.

As the presents kept coming, Jesse began to

think, *This baby hasn't even been born yet and already it's spoiled rotten.*

"I still feel bad we don't have a baby shower gift," said Daisy. She placed the beach ball with the rest of the presents.

"I kind of think it already has enough stuff," said Jesse. "Hey, wait! I have a great idea. Let's sing it a song. We'll sing it 'The Sail Song.'"

"Brilliant!" said Daisy.

And so, when Jesse and Daisy saw a gap in the parade of gift-givers, they swam up before the abalone shell and, on the count of three, started singing "The Sail Song." Yar, catching on quickly, joined in. Soon, others were singing along, too. And when the song was over, the water fizzed and bubbled with cheering.

Jesse leaned into the abalone shell and gently pushed aside the seaweed quilt someone had just brought. He wanted to see if the egg was vibrating to show its appreciation of their gift.

But the egg wasn't vibrating. The egg, in fact, wasn't an egg at all. It was a soggy softball, the same one that had been swiped from Jesse's bunk-side table in the middle of the night. Jesse felt himself heat up with anger.

"What's wrong, Jess?" Daisy asked.

"The egg is gone!" he said in a choked whisper.

"What's that you say?" said Yar in a loud voice. "The egg is gone, you say?" He swam up to the shell and picked up the softball, crushing it in his fins. He held it on high, his arm trembling. "THE EGG IS GONE!" Yar's booming voice rang out and was immediately followed by a hundred echoes of "The egg is gone!"

What came next was what could only be described as underwater pandemonium. Mermothers clutched their babies to their breasts, selkies howled and kelpies whinnied, and everyone milled about, churning up the sand and clouding the waters.

Yar cleared his throat loudly and shouted over the din, "No one is to exit this portal without undergoing a thorough search from head to fins, from claw to swimmeret! Everyone, line up and present yourselves to the bull sharks at the door!"

The other shark shivers joined together to form a ring around the guests.

Through all the chaos, Emmy hovered over the abalone shell, staring down into it. "It's no use, Yar!" she called out at length.

"You too, miss!" said Yar. "There can be no exceptions to the rule."

"I mean *it's too late*," Emmy explained. "The eagle has left the barn."

"The saying is either the horse has left the barn or the eagle has landed," Jesse said.

"What I'm trying to tell all of you is that it's TOO LATE! The slippery scoundrels have already made off with the egg!" Emmy said.

"What slippery scoundrels?" Daisy asked.

"I thought there was something a little fishy about those two," Emmy went on.

"What two?" said Jesse.

"The two mermen who brought the baby quilt. But I was too impressed by their jeweled masks and their gold mesh capes to act on my hunch," Emmy said, wagging her head. "And now look at it." She pointed into the shell. Where the brightly colored quilt had lain there was now a tattered rag and a puddle of goop that looked like an oil spill.

"You mean those two mermen in jeweled masks and golden cloaks who brought it . . . ?" Fluke asked.

Yar swam up and inspected the mess. "Dash it all! Red Eyes! Those masks and cloaks concealed their red-rimmed eyes and their sickly green pallor from us," he said with a sorry shake of his head. "I should have known!"

"After all this time, you'd think we'd be wise to their tricks," said Fluke. She called out to the sharks, "Release the guests!" Then she turned to

Emmy and the Keepers. "Shall we go and discuss a game plan?"

The five of them shucked off their jewelry and slipped into the stream of guests exiting the molly-coddle.

Jesse and Daisy swam on either side of Emmy. They both tried to gauge Emmy's state of mind, but her green eyes were unreadable. When they arrived up on deck, they hovered around the table. Fluke's noble head drooped so low her nose grazed the surface of the table.

"Buck up, Cap'n," said Yar. "No need for self-recrimination. I'll grant you, this is a most unfortunate turn of events, but it could have happened on anyone's watch."

"But it happened on *mine,* Chief," said Fluke despondently. "I'll go down in the books as the captain on whose watch the dragon egg was lost."

Yar nodded sagely. "I fear we made the mistake of counting our dragon before it hatched, as it were. And now it looks as if Maldew has scored the ultimate win."

"This is Maldew's doing?" Jesse asked.

"Oh, yes. It's most definitely the Mermage's point," said Fluke.

"You keep talking like this is some kind of a game," Jesse said.

"Ra*ther*," Yar agreed. "And a thumping good one it has been, too, kicked off by our ancestors that fateful day when they first came upon the egg lying on that sandbar in aught-nine. Since then, the egg has been passed back and forth between our teams, what? Hundreds of times, it must be. But it appears that, given the imminent advent of the dragon's hatching, the ultimate victory is to fall to Maldew. Double drat!"

Emmy, who had been listening to this exchange in moody silence, spoke up in a low, determined voice. "Jesse Tiger's right. This is *not* a game!"

Fluke and Yar stared at her in perplexity. "It's not?" they chimed.

"This is my own dragon flesh and blood we're talking about here. Not a soccer ball or a football or a hockey puck. And it's a fact that if that dragon hatches in the possession of the Mermage, he or she will be bound to serve the Mermage for all of its days."

"Grim business, what?" said Yar, tugging at his whiskers anxiously.

"How do you know that?" Jesse asked Emmy.

"Because my mother told me that's the way it works," said Emmy. "I hatched in your possession and I serve you, don't I?"

Jesse and Daisy swapped skeptical looks. Daisy

said, "We kind of thought it was the other way around, Em: that we served you."

"I scratch your head. You scratch mine," Emmy said.

"I think it's back," said Jesse.

"Head, back, butt, what difference does it make? If my baby sib winds up serving the Mermage, the Mermage's power will be magnified to the nth power."

"What's the nth power?" Jesse asked.

"About a bazillion times," Emmy said. "Dragons are only as good as the master they serve. Maldew is bad, so he will use this dragon to make himself even more powerful and more evil. Not only will he rule the Eighth Sea, but he'll take over the other seven as well.

"And as Scuppers the Sage, the wisest selkie who ever swam the Eight, once said, 'Whosoever rules the Eight Seas, rules all four realms.'"

"*That* would be very bad," said Jesse.

"So where do we find Mildew?" Emmy asked.

"That's *Maldew*, old girl," said Yar.

"Mildew, Maldew, moldy old honeydew," said Emmy. "Where does this Mermage hang out?"

"Why, in the Coral Jungle, of course," said Fluke.

The cousins and Emmy looked at one another.

"I knew that, sooner or later, we'd have to go back to that malankey place," said Daisy, heaving a heavy sigh.

"Well, then, what are we waiting for?" Emmy said. "The ball—I mean, the egg—is in play until the dragon hatches, and I, for one, intend to play until the last. If this is a game, it's a game we're playing for keeps, a game we are going to win. The best defense is a strong offense, I always say. So what do you say, Team Emerald?" Emmy held out her right arm.

Jesse and Daisy piled their hands on top of her giant claw. "We're in," said Daisy.

"Big-time," said Jesse. "Coral Jungle or bust."

Fluke sputtered, "B-but you can't just swim in there. As far as we know, no one who's ever gone in there has ever come out as anything but a Red Eyes."

"We'll go in," Emmy said firmly, "and we'll come out just fine."

"I have no doubt you'll fit right in as a dragon fish," said Fluke. "But what about Jesse and Daisy? They're White Eyes."

Jesse and Daisy turned to Emmy.

Emmy said, "Yes, but they'll look like Red Eyes after I've rubbed them down with dragon ichor."

"What's that?" Jesse asked.

"Isn't that the slimy vegetable they put in gumbo?" Daisy said.

"I think that's okra," said Jesse.

"*Ichor* is a magical substance I secrete through the ends of my talons," Emmy said. "It has many uses."

Jesse looked at Daisy and shrugged. They had known Emmy her whole life, but she was still full of surprises.

"Since when?" Jesse asked.

"Since the salt water drew it out," Emmy said. "You got tails and gills. I got ichor. Come here, Keepers, and get your ichor." As if she were extracting lotion from a tube, Emmy retracted her claws and then pushed them out again. Something that looked like bright green ink shot out the ends of her talons and covered her paws. Pulling in her talons again, Emmy rubbed Jesse's and Daisy's human halves. When she was finished, they glowed as green as the Incredible Hulk.

"Remarkable!" said Fluke.

"Uncanny," said Yar.

"Except we don't have red eyes," Daisy pointed out.

"True," said Emmy. "I could give you red-rimmed, bloodshot eyes but it might blind you for life."

"That's okay. We're good," said Jesse with an uneasy laugh.

"Maybe you could borrow some sunglasses from the big pile in the Lost and Found cabin?" Emmy suggested.

"Brilliant!" said Daisy.

"Jolly good thinking, that," said Yar. She reached out for a passing eel and brought Star forth with a loud *zzzzt*.

Yar and Fluke explained the plan to her. She bustled off belowdecks and returned with some white-framed Foster Grants for Jesse and a snazzy pair with blue rhinestone frames for Daisy. Star had chosen a pair of glamorous black wraparounds for herself.

"Why the dark glasses, Star, old gal?" Yar asked.

Star pulled herself up boldly. "Because I'm going with them. Request permission to leave the ship."

Chapter Nine

A STAR TO GUIDE THEM

"This is most irregular," said Fluke.

"The Keepers and Emmy will need someone to guide them to the Coral Jungle," Star said.

"You know it's not safe to leave the ship!" Fluke said.

"Actually," said Star, her chin held high, "I do it all the time. I'll be fine."

Fluke and Yar dealt her a stern look.

"I've even gone into the jungle once or twice," Star said, "on a double-dare from my friends."

"I beg your pardon?" Yar said, swelling up with outrage.

"But mostly we ride the waves," Star added meekly. "Anyway, I know the safest way in. I can be as useful to them as I am to you . . . but in a different way."

Yar and Fluke swam off a short distance and whispered back and forth. After they had arrived at an agreement, they swam back.

"Permission granted," Fluke said finally.

"Thank you!" Star said, throwing her arms around Fluke's shoulders and hugging her, then doing the same to Yar.

Yar pulled away and tugged nervously at his whiskers. "Do take care, though. It's fiendishly dangerous out there. Still, I imagine the dragon will protect you from harm."

"No sweat, mateys," said Emmy.

Yar said, "I suppose we'll simply have to make do on our own without you for the duration. Might try swabbing the deck myself, what?"

After Emmy rubbed Star down with dragon

ichor and turned her every bit as green as she had the Keepers, the four made ready to set out in the direction of the Coral Jungle.

Word of their journey must have spread among the passengers of *The Golden Dragon,* for the decks were soon thronged with well-wishers—selkies and merfolk and kelpies and even a few polar bears—waving sea fans and hanks of seaweed.

Before the party took their leave, Fluke presented them each with a conch shell well stocked with phosphairies. "They say the Coral Jungle is a dark and murky place. A little illumination will come in handy," she said.

"Thanks. But won't the phosphairies be in danger?" Daisy asked.

"No worries," said Emmy as she rubbed each conch shell until it shone bright green. "Now they'll pass for mini water zombies. Either that or tiny traffic lights. And speaking of green lights," she said, "let's get going before my sib hatches into the lair of the Mermage and the Eight Seas turn into one great big seething zombie pit."

"*Rather!*" said Yar. "Best be moving along, then, what?"

A group of water sprites mounted on dolphins swam alongside the party as far as the rock near the bright orange fan coral where Daisy had stopped to rake the kelp out of her hair. As the escort spun around and rode back to the ship, the four travelers turned toward the curtain of blackness that loomed in the distance.

Now that they knew the evil Mermage Maldew dwelled in the heart of the Coral Jungle, it seemed all the more ominous to them as they swam steadily toward it. The tortured tangle of coral all but reached out to pull them into its murky depths.

They came to the edge of the jungle and halted. What looked like a large cave loomed before them.

"This bald area is where we usually sneak in," Star said. "Me and Coral and Reef."

"I don't get it. Why would you come here if you didn't have to?" Daisy asked.

"Because it's fun!" Star said with a delighted shiver.

"Really?" said Daisy.

"Sure, Daise," said Jesse. "Scary fun. Like that abandoned, haunted house up on Old Mine Road."

Daisy nodded slowly. "I guess. Let's go and have ourselves some scary fun," she said, twirling her finger without enthusiasm.

Star said, "Okay, but first, I have to do our nails."

"A *manicure*? Now?" Daisy asked. "You've got to be kidding."

Star picked up a sea sponge and, saturating it with a blob of sticky tar that was floating in the water, began to rub Daisy's fingernails until they turned black. Then she did the same with Jesse's.

"It's a *mud*-icure!" Jesse said, holding up his black-nailed fingers and wiggling them ghoulishly.

"Close attention to the details is always important, as any good mer-maid knows," Star said with a pert little nod of her head. "Oh, and one final word. When you see a Red Eye, just wave but don't let them touch you."

"How come?" Jesse said. "Not that I'd want to."

"If they touch you three times, you'll become one of them," Star said.

"How do you know that?" Daisy asked.

"Coral and Reef told me," Star said. "We play a game called Red Eye Tag. Three tags and you're Red."

"Yeah, but how come Reef and Coral know this?" Jesse asked.

Star shrugged. "My friends know tons of stuff. Oh, and stay clear of the black coral. That stuff stings."

"I already learned that the hard way," Daisy said, showing Star the white welt on her finger.

"What about the other creatures in the Coral Jungle?" Jesse asked. "Are they dangerous, too?"

"What other creatures?" Star said. "Everything and everyone else moved out a long time ago. Only merfolk are vulnerable to Maldew's power."

"Good to know, since we just happen to be in the form of merfolk," Jesse said slowly. "Anything else we need to know before we take the plunge?"

"Act creepy," said Emmy.

"Creepy, right," said Jesse. "I am a water zombie." He held out his arms limply before him. "Are you going to act creepy, Emmy?"

"I'm going to transform into a dragon fish," said Emmy, doing exactly that.

"I'd say that's creepy," said Daisy; then, with a roll of her eyes, she added, "She was *so* much cuter as a sheepdog."

Emmy flashed her needles at them in a cunning fashion and turned toward the Coral Jungle.

Lanterns hoisted, with Emmy leading the way, the cousins and Star swam slowly into the jungle.

The water felt instantly warmer and not in a comfortable and relaxing way. If looking at the Coral Jungle from the outside was a creepy proposition, being in the thick of it was far creepier. The sunglasses made it difficult to see through the cloudy water. It even smelled bad, worse than the sea at low tide, like wash water in which dirty socks and dead fish had been soaking. As they followed along behind Emmy, the Keepers and Star kept their arms tucked in close to their bodies and tried to move their tails as little as possible to avoid grazing the black coral. The jungle seemed deserted.

"Where is everybody?" Jesse wondered.

"At the Mermage's hideout?" Daisy suggested.

"Where's that, do you think?" Jesse asked.

"I guess we just keep swimming until we see something that looks like a Mermage's hideout," said Star. "My friends and I always stick to the outskirts. I've never gone in this deep before."

"If we see someone, maybe we should just stop them and ask them directions," said Daisy.

"I think the less contact we have with the Red Eyes, the safer we'll be," said Jesse.

"Ess," said Emmy.

Green faces began to appear out of the gloom, mere yards away, raising limp arms toward them in melancholy salutation.

Jesse and Daisy and Star lifted limp arms and returned the greeting. If the Red Eyes wondered why anyone would need sunglasses in such a dark place, they gave no sign.

A few moments later, Emmy shimmied to a halt. Then she shooed them behind a wide trunk of black coral just as a heft of six beefy Red Eyes with heads full of swirling braids and wielding rusty tridents swam past.

"Oh, my scales and fins!" Star cried out, and clapped a hand over her mouth.

"What is it?" Daisy asked her.

"The Red Eyes. I recognize one of them. It's Rock. He was my friend," Star said sadly.

"Well, I hate to tell you, but he's not your friend anymore," said Jesse.

"Ollow em!" said Emmy.

By which the others understood her to mean, "Follow them," and this is what they did at a safe distance. It was a good thing, too, because the burly shoulders of the Red Eyes cut a nice broad swath through the stinging coral.

As Emmy and the merkids increased their speed to keep up with the squad, Jesse found himself wondering what the Mermage would look like. Would he be a hulking merman with a head full of long tight braids and green skin holding a trident? Or would he have a magic wand? In their time as Dragon Keepers, Jesse and Daisy had faced off with St. George the Dragon Slayer and his consort Sadra the Witch. Those two looked like humans, only a lot scarier. They had also battled thuggish Fire Dragons, dogs spelled into knights in armor, and large mad dogs and acid-spewing fire lions. So how bad, really, could an underwater sorcerer really be?

Eventually, the heft of Red Eyes swam into a wide clearing, where the seafloor was as black and scorched-looking as a forest after a raging fire had swept through it. In the center of the clearing lay an object twice the size of a semitrailer: long and green and slimy-looking and covered with red bristles. The Red Eyes swam up to one end of the long green thing, from which a steady line of bubbles streamed. Daisy wondered if the Mermage was hidden somewhere inside the green thing.

Jesse, thinking along the same lines, said, "This must be the Mermage's hideout."

"I don't think so," said Star in a low voice. "I remember that Reef and Coral said something about Maldew being a giant sea cucumber. I thought it was a joke, but—"

"Holy moly!" Jesse said. "You mean to say that the big-deal Mermage Maldew is really just a humungous sea cucumber?"

"That just might be the grossest thing I've ever seen," said Daisy with a deep shudder.

"Well, if that's him," said Jesse, "at least he can't move very fast. I'm pretty sure sea cucumbers have minimal powers of movement. Let's get a little closer to him so we can check him out. Those bubbles are probably where his lips are. Or the closest thing a sea cucumber has to lips."

Jesse started to swim out into the clearing.

"No, Jesse, don't!" Star cried out.

But it was too late. One of the Red Eyes had turned away from the giant sea cucumber and seen Jesse.

"Uh-oh," said Emmy.

"Who goes there?" the Red Eyes called out.

The other five Red Eyes turned to look; then they all swam over and bore down upon the trespassers.

"How dare you enter the Mermage's Inner Circle!" one of them said.

The Red Eyes were even more imposing up close. Unlike the other Red Eyes they had seen, these didn't have limp arms and lifeless voices. Perhaps, Jesse thought, being the Mermage's guards gave them special strength and powers. The green skin of these Red Eyes bulged with muscles and their red-rimmed, bloodshot eyes were more angry than vacant. Through clenched teeth, they growled low and wove back and forth like grizzly bears on their hind legs working up to an attack.

"Rock? Is that you?" Star said to the smallest of the Red Eyes. "It's me. Star. Your old friend. You probably don't recognize me with these glasses."

"Whatever you do, *do not* take off your sunglasses," Jesse said to her out of the corner of his mouth.

Rock replied in a flat voice, "I recognize only my master."

Star pinched her lips together, bowed her head, and looked as if she were holding back tears. When she raised her head again, she said to her companions, "If we get out of this alive, I'm never leaving the ship again!"

"Ay alm," said Emmy.

But it was hard to stay calm with twenty-four rusty trident points aimed at them. With those tridents, the Red Eyes began to prod them toward the bubbling mouth of the Mermage.

Emmy's red dragon fish scales had begun to blanch as she flitted to keep clear of the trident points, which were made of iron.

Daisy, realizing this, spoke up. "Keep those things away from our dragon fish!"

One of them jabbed the trident menacingly at Daisy. As she dodged it, her sunglasses fell off and tumbled to the seafloor. She tried to grab them back but the same Red Eyes picked them up in his fist and growled at her, "You're a White Eyes!"

The other Red Eyes all turned to stare at Daisy.

In a show of solidarity, Jesse whipped off his sunglasses, followed by Star.

"They're all White Eyes!" the Red Eyes snarled as he prodded Jesse, Daisy, and Star closer to the bubbling end of the sea cucumber. Here, the water was even warmer and more rank-smelling.

"We bring you three fresh White Eyes, Master," the Red Eyes said. He was the biggest and burliest, and he seemed to be the leader.

Apart from the quivering mass of red bristles that covered his body and a slight puckering at the end, the creature the Red Eyes called master was nearly featureless. A series of big bubbles that smelled like sewage burst in the captives' faces. Sounding like a giant wheezing fat man gargling oil, a voice asked, "What do the White Eyes want?"

Jesse said the first thing that popped into his head. "Nothing. We just want to get out of this place. We're lost."

Daisy said, "We took a wrong turn."

"YOU LIE!" the Mermage bellowed. A stream of foul-smelling bubbles drove the four backward, choking and coughing. But the Red Eyes behind them prodded them again, forcing them back toward the Mermage.

The Mermage went on in a more subdued tone.

"Belleweather sent you. This feels like one of her tricks."

"Her?" Daisy snorted. "Captain Belleweather's not a female."

Jesse nudged Daisy and whispered, "Um, Daise? I think she might be."

"What are you talking about, Jess?" she whispered back.

"Last night, I was going to tell you but I fell asleep." And then Jesse told Daisy, all in a rush, about the crystal ball and Mitzi Driftwood waving the sizzling marshmallow stick over him. It wasn't the place to tell her something this important but it was high time. "And she was the one who gave us the spelled seashells, wasn't she? So it kind of adds up. Daise, Mitzi Driftwood *is* Captain Belleweather."

"But Belleweather is a selkie, like Yar, and she looks like a human woman . . . in a black wet suit," Daisy said, falling silent while she added it all up in her head. When she finished, her eyes nearly popped out of her head. "Jesse!" she cried. "You're right! Belleweather *did* send us!"

CHAPTER TEN

THE WRATH OF THE MERMAGE

Daisy turned to the Mermage and said, "So how come Belleweather's a beach beauty and you're a hideously ugly sea cucumber?"

The sea cucumber's bristles quivered and it started to swell up.

"Oh, no!" said Star, shrinking away. "You've gotten him angry now."

A storm of rotten-egg bubbles burst in their faces.

Daisy waved them away. "Maybe if he gets mad enough, he'll answer my question," she said.

Jesse, getting the idea, joined in. "Yeah, we didn't realize that the great Maldew was a lowly sea cucumber. From all the stories we heard on board *The Golden Dragon,* we thought you were going to be this magnificent merman."

The Mermage continued to swell up until he looked like an enormous blowfish.

"Oh, you've done it now," said Star, covering her head as the water all around the swollen sea cucumber bubbled.

The Mermage began to speak. "I was the most magnificent merman in the Eighth Sea . . . until that sea witch trounced me."

"Really?" Jesse said, continuing to bait the beast. "You let yourself be beat by a woman?"

Angry bubbles burst all around them like stink bombs. "We both wanted the dragon egg. One night, she whipped up a lightning storm the likes of which I have never seen. Belleweather was up on the bridge of *The Golden Dragon* when I rose from the boiling sea and scuttled her precious ship with a stab of my trident." Like leaks through pinholes in a balloon, Maldew's words gradually reduced his size.

Daisy nudged Jesse. "He's right," she said. "I saw three holes in the hull of *The Golden Dragon*!"

Jesse turned back to the Mermage. "A little trident sinking a mighty ship like the *Dragon*? Like the measly ones your guards have?" Jesse said, pointing to the Red Eyes. "I bet you're exaggerating."

"I assure you, White Eyes, my trident is most powerful and still is," Maldew said in a deadly quiet voice. "But Belleweather was fast. She struck me with a lightning bolt that turned me into sea sludge."

"Ick," Daisy said.

"As *The Golden Dragon* sank, so did I, to the bottom of the sea. I would have remained there, a powerless puddle of ooze, had I not had the good fortune to settle into the body of a sea cucumber. I was able to inhabit that sea cucumber and survive."

"You call being turned into a sea slug *lucky*?" Jesse said with a sneer.

"What does a puny White Eyes know of luck . . . or power? I actually began to thrive in my new state, swelling to my current impressive proportions. The Coral Jungle grew up around me, and all merfolk who swim into it come under my power and do my bidding . . . as you three soon will."

"You mean only merpeople can fall under your power?" Daisy said. "That means you can't control Belleweather because she's a selkie."

"Ah, but I do, in a way. My last act before I turned to sludge was to cast a spell on her that made her fall in love with the first lubber she laid eyes on. A daredevil surfer happened to paddle out into the midst of the storm that night. He saw Belleweather and thought he was saving her."

"How romantic," Daisy said, and meant it.

"Selkies who fall in love with mortals sacrifice some of their power, if only because they must live on the land to be with their lubber mates. It has kept her, for the most part, out of my way. And the remaining White Eyes have had to fend for themselves, pack of fools and knaves that you are, huddling on board Belleweather's sunken ship. But now the dragon egg is in my possession and about to hatch. When the dragon hatches, I will harness its power to blight the White Eyes and all the other creatures of the Eighth Sea . . . but I will save Belleweather and her half-breed spawn for last."

Emmy hissed, long and low.

Maldew spoke to the Red Eyes next. "Take

them and lay hands on them until their eyes are as red as my anger is hot."

Star let out a shriek as the heft of Red Eyes began to close in on them again. Just then, Emmy transformed from a fish into a dragon. The Red Eyes fell back, cowering.

"By the Great Red Tide, you're a full-blown dragon!" Maldew said in wonder.

Feet planted in the black sand, Emmy's green eyes blazed. "I've come for the egg. Where is it, Maldew?"

Everything happened very quickly after that. The six Red Eyes raised their tridents and drove them, tines first, deep into the sand. Maldew sucked in great quantities of seawater through his puckered mouth. Emmy snatched up Jesse, Daisy, and Star and kept them from being pulled into Maldew's maw. Along with water, all manner of objects came flying through the jungle from all directions toward Maldew—ships' anchors and chains, spearguns, rusted pilings, and even an ancient diving helmet. All this flotsam and jetsam came to be plastered across the Mermage's body like iron filings on the end of a giant magnet. The more objects that ac-cumulated, the weaker Emmy grew, until she dropped first Jesse, then Daisy, and finally Star. The dragon began to shrink slowly until she was once again a dragon fish, a pale and sickly-looking dragon fish, foaming at the mouth.

The Mermage stopped sucking and the water went still, except for the clinking of the pieces of scrap metal, rubbing against each other among his bristles.

"What happened to your dragon?" Star asked in a trembling voice.

"All this stuff is made of iron," Jesse said.

"It was too much for her," Daisy said sadly.

The Red Eyes lifted their tridents out of the sand and swam forth. One of them pried the ancient diving helmet off of Maldew's body and clapped it down on the seafloor over Emmy, trapping her. She peered out miserably from the round glass window, her fins barely moving.

Maldew exhaled a long, malodorous breath and sent all the metal drifting away from him to settle around the diving helmet, thus trapping Emmy even more surely.

"Now, where was I?" said Maldew. "Oh, yes. I was ordering the White Eyes to be made *Red*."

The Red Eyes pressed in upon the three captives.

"Dive between them and swim for it!" Star whispered frantically.

"It's no use," said Jesse. "We'd never make it. And we can't leave Emmy."

"Wait a minute!" Daisy cried out to Maldew. "It would be a big mistake to turn us into Red Eyes. You can use us. We happen to be fully qualified dragon doulas!"

Maldew called off the Red Eyes, who obediently pulled back.

"Speak, White Eyes!" Maldew bellowed. "And I caution you not to make me more angry than I already am."

Daisy swallowed hard. "You need us, Maldew, to assist in the hatching of this dragon," she said. "We're experts. Dragon hatchings are very complicated. If something goes wrong, your dragon may be less than healthy. A less-than-healthy dragon has very little chance of surviving, and if it does, it will possess very weak magic. I'm surprised you don't know that, a wise and powerful Mermage like yourself."

Jesse worked to keep a straight face. No one told a whopper better than his cousin.

"Why should I believe a White Eyes?" Maldew said.

"Because it's the truth," Daisy said. "Show us where the egg is, Maldew, before something truly terrible happens."

"I'd listen to her if I were you," said Jesse.

The water around the sea cucumber went black and foul with tiny little bubbles as he mulled this over. Finally, words came out. "Very well. Take the White Eyes to the tugboat," Maldew said to the Red Eyes.

To Jesse, Daisy, and Star he added, "But know this, White Eyes. If anything happens to the dragon during the hatching, I will hold you personally responsible. And the consequences will be unspeakable."

The heft of Red Eyes surrounded them and began to prod them away from the clearing and back into the jungle.

Jesse cast one last backward glance at the diving helmet holding Emmy. Then he swam up even with Star and whispered in her ear, "Try and escape. Swim to the beach and tell Reef and Coral we need help."

Star nodded. After they had been swimming through the jungle for some time, she whispered to Jesse and Daisy, "Cover your eyes."

Jesse and Daisy did as bidden. No sooner had they done so than there was a huge explosion of bright green light. The Red Eyes pulled back, shielding their eyes.

When the explosion of light subsided, an empty conch shell lay where Star had been.

"Go, Star, go!" Daisy chanted under her breath.

Star had released the phosphairies from her conch shell. The sudden surge of green light had temporarily blinded the Red Eyes and enabled Star to make her getaway.

While the Red Eyes rubbed their red eyes, Jesse shooed the loose phosphairies into his and Daisy's conch shells.

As soon as the Red Eyes had regained their sight, they began to argue amongst themselves as Jesse and Daisy looked on, hoping they quibbled long enough to give Star time to swim away.

"Two of us can chase down the runaway," one of the Red Eyes said.

"I'll go with Rock," said another, "and we'll get her."

"No, let her go. We must follow the master's orders," said the burliest Red Eye. "The egg needs tending first. Whoever doesn't agree with me, raise a hand."

"I'm with Marino," a Red Eyes said, raising his hand.

Marino's burning eyes swept over the other four and, one by one, much to Jesse's and Daisy's relief, they raised their hands, voting not to chase after Star.

Marino nodded, then turned to Jesse and Daisy and brandished his trident. "You two. Get moving."

They continued their swim through the Coral Jungle. At length they came upon the sunken carcass of an old tugboat. Four more beefy Red Eyes armed with tridents guarded the pilot's cabin, whose windows were crusted over with blackened barnacles.

"Open up," Marino said to the nearest guard.

The guard opened the door, and the Red Eye escort crowded in on Jesse and Daisy and forced them into the cabin, shutting the door behind them.

It was a good thing Jesse and Daisy still had their phosphairy lanterns, for they lit up the small, dark space. The water inside the tugboat cabin was as intensely warm as bathwater right out of the hot water tap. There was black kelp strewn everywhere. On the chart table, nestled in Jesse and Daisy's backpack, lay the Thunder Egg.

At first, it looked like the egg was swaying with the current of the sea. But when they swam closer, Jesse and Daisy saw that it was rocking steadily back and forth under its own power.

Slowly, they set their conch shells on either side of the backpack. The phosphairies swarmed out of the shells, as if they, too, wanted to get a better look.

"Look, Jess," Daisy whispered, pointing.

In the green light of the hovering phosphairies, they saw that a small crack had formed in one side of the egg.

Gingerly, Jesse touched the egg. "Hot!" he said, pulling back. It reminded him of the red-hot doorknob of his bedroom, right before Emmy's egg had gone *kablam* in the sock drawer.

"Oh, boy," he said. "What happens if it explodes the way Emmy's egg did and we're here in the cabin with it? We could get blown to bits."

Daisy nibbled at her cuticle. "Maybe that won't happen underwater. Maybe water will soften the impact."

"And maybe not," said Jesse.

"Maybe not," Daisy agreed glumly.

Now that Daisy's plan had gotten them this far, they were both at a loss as to what to do next. Besides, it was almost too hot in the cabin to think.

"This hot water is making me drowsy," said Daisy. "What about you?"

"Yeah, it's like being in a hot tub," Jesse said.

"It's probably past bedtime now, don't you think?" Daisy said.

"It's hard to tell down here," Jesse said.

"But it *feels* late, doesn't it?" Daisy said.

Jesse nodded. It felt late and he was hungry and homesick. The phrase popped into his mind: *seasick*. So he said it out loud. "I think I'm seasick."

"You mean dizzy and sick to your stomach?" Daisy asked.

"No, sick of the sea," said Jesse. "And really, really tired."

"It would be bad for us to fall asleep," Daisy said.

There was a pile of razor clams on the floor of the cabin. Jesse got one for himself and handed one to Daisy. "Try sticking yourself with the sharp edge to stay alert."

"Good idea," said Daisy.

Whenever they felt themselves start to drop off, they would squeeze their shells and snap awake. But soon, the urge to sleep was too powerful to resist any longer. They were each vaguely aware of their hands opening, of the razor clamshells floating away, of their bodies going limp as they drifted off to sleep, floating, like astronauts in a capsule that was lost in space.

Daisy woke up first with a sudden snort. Bubbles streamed out of her nose. She looked around for Jesse and found him floating up by the ceiling, snoring away in his own cloud of bubbles.

Then she heard a steady thumping noise.

At first, she thought it was the egg, getting ever nearer to hatching. She swam over and examined it carefully. The crack wasn't any bigger. It was still rocking slowly back and forth, but not vigorously enough to be making such a loud knocking sound.

Daisy reached up and tugged Jesse's tail, dragging him back down toward the floor.

"What? What?" he said, opening his eyes wide and shaking his head. "I was just resting."

"Hear that?" Daisy said, holding up a finger.

Jesse listened, nodding. The thumping sound was even louder now.

"Don't worry. It's not the Thunder Egg," she said.

"But what is it?" Jesse said. He swam over to the window and peered through a small clearing in the encrusted barnacles. A Red Eyes cruised past, followed by another and another. They were patrolling the pilot's cabin, ceaselessly swimming, like a shiver of sharks, but none of them was touching the cabin. "Nothing much happening out there," he said.

The noise seemed to be coming from the floor of the pilothouse. Daisy swam down and pulled aside a mass of black kelp, revealing a square trapdoor.

"What's under there, I wonder?" Daisy asked.

"Beats me," Jesse said. "Maybe the motor?"

"I think the knocking's coming from in there," she said. "Could the motor be switched on?"

"Only one way to find out." Jesse swam to the trapdoor. There was a small hook on one side of it. He put his finger in and lifted the door.

Coral Driftwood, with a bright green face and red-rimmed eyes, swam up into the cabin.

CHAPTER ELEVEN

PLAY BALL!

"Look out, she's a Red Eyes!" Jesse cried, grabbing Daisy and swimming away from Coral.

"Yeah, right," said Coral. She winked at them and gave her seashell necklace a little tug. "Hey, dudes! What took you so long? I've been knocking on that hatch forever. I thought you'd never come. Star sent me."

"You mean you're not a Red Eyes?" Jesse said meekly.

"About as much as you are a merboy," Coral said. "Did I wake you up?"

"As a matter of fact," Daisy confessed sheepishly, "we fell asleep."

"I don't blame you!" Coral said. "It's hot as Davy Jones's mud bath down here."

"How did you know where to find us?" Daisy asked.

"Star said they were taking you to a tug," Coral answered. "This is the only tug down here. Best part about it is the nice big gaping hole in the aft hull." Coral swam over and looked at the egg, an expression of awe on her face. She didn't have a fish tail, but she did have gills behind her ears and her feet ended in fins that hadn't come from any diving store.

Coral turned to Jesse and Daisy and said, "It's getting close to hatching, isn't it?"

"We think so," said Daisy. "It can't be moved. Besides, it's too hot to handle."

"Dudes, it *has* to be moved," Coral said. "My mom says that if the egg hatches in the Coral Jungle, it will be stillborn, which would be a world-class bummer. So we *have* to get it out. We can handle it. I came prepared." She opened a pouch on her belt and pulled out a bulky silver mitt, the heavy-duty kind made for lifting piping-hot pans out of the oven.

"Where did you get that?" Jesse asked.

"Dude, where else? From our kitchen," Coral said.

"That beach shack actually has a kitchen?" Daisy said.

Coral leveled her blue eyes at them. "You have no idea what gnarly wonders that sugar shack holds," she said. "You've been on *The Golden Dragon,* right?"

Jesse and Daisy nodded.

"Well, then, imagine what my mom can fit into a beach shack in the side of a cliff."

"Wow," said Jesse. "I want to play at *your* house after school."

"My mom's powers are bangin'. But enough talk. Let's book. We can leave the way I came in."

"Won't the Red Eyes see us?" Daisy asked.

"I doubt it. They've got their beady little red-rimmed eyes glued to the pilothouse. They'll never know we've left until we're long gone. Come on, if we don't show up soon, my mom will worry and she doesn't need the agg."

"How did you make your face green and your eyes red?" Daisy asked. "Magic?"

Coral snorted with mirth. "No, waterproof makeup."

"Wait!" said Jesse. "We can't leave."

"You heard her, Jess," said Daisy. "The egg's in immediate danger."

"Emmy's in just as much danger and we can't leave her down here," Jesse said.

"Who's Emmy?" Coral asked.

"Our dragon," Jesse and Daisy said together.

"You dudes have a dragon?" Coral asked. "Like an already hatched one?"

"Six months old and as big as two elephants," Daisy said.

"That sneaky little Star never said anything about *another* dragon," Coral said.

"Yeah, well," said Jesse, "Maldew's got her trapped in a diving helmet."

"Cowabunga! That must be some big diving helmet!" Coral said.

"It's a long story," said Jesse.

"Two dragons in trouble at the same time!" said Daisy, wagging her head. "What are we going to do?"

"Okay, okay, let's all just try and keep it real,"

said Coral, looking from one cousin to the next, then returning to Jesse. "Dude, you look like the Man with the Plan."

"Well, as a matter of fact . . ." Jesse smiled slowly, reaching into the pouch of his sweatshirt. The softball was still there. He had retrieved it from the abalone shell after the mollycoddle. He took out the softball now and showed it to Coral and Daisy. "Dudettes," he said to them, "it's time to play ball."

They put their heads together and, by the light of the swarming phosphairies, plotted out their plan as quickly as they could, knowing how pressed for time they were. When they were finished, Coral carefully picked up the real egg and held it in the oven mitt.

Jesse said, "I'll take the backpack. You're going to be okay here alone, Daise?" It was less a question than a hope.

"Totally," Daisy said. "I have my trusty phony Thunder Egg, don't I?" She pointed to the softball, which was now nestled in place of the real egg in the center of an old life preserver.

"Take this, too," Jesse said. He removed their grandfather's boatswain's pipe from around his neck and draped it around hers.

"Remember what Polly told us," Jesse said. "Should you happen to find yourself beset by perils, blow on it good and hard: one long burst, two short ones. Help, in some shape or form, is bound to come a-running."

"Got it," said Daisy.

"Think you'll remember how to use it if the time comes?" he asked.

"I'll be fine, Jess. You guys need to go on and git before that egg hatches. Take the phosphairies with you."

As if hearing their cue, the phosphairies swam back into the conch shells. Daisy watched Jesse and Coral swim slowly down through the trapdoor into pitch darkness through which the conch shell lanterns cut two bright green swaths. Then she lowered the hatch and got busy. First she arranged a pile of kelp until it looked like the body of Jesse sleeping in a heap; then she got a razor clam.

"Sorry, ball," she said to the softball as she sliced a jagged hole in one side of it. Then she went to the cabin door and pounded on it.

When Rock opened the door, Daisy was holding the "egg" in a swaddling of kelp. "Finally!" she said.

Rock peered into the cabin behind her. Without the phosphairies, the cabin was dark. Daisy indicated the mound of kelp in one corner. "The White

Eyes is seasick," she said. "He needs to be left alone."

Rock's eyes widened in confusion.

"Go and tell Maldew his egg is about to hatch. He won't want to miss it," Daisy said firmly.

Rock stammered, "But . . . but . . ."

"But *nothing*, Rock!" Daisy barked at him. "We need to get Maldew over here pronto, before this egg cracks wide open."

"But Maldew can't move!" Rock sputtered.

"What's going on here!" Marino swam up, shouldering Rock aside.

"She says the egg is hatching soon," Rock said. "Maldew must see it."

"Let me see," Marino said.

"Stay back!" Daisy held the kelp-swaddled ball to her chest. "It might hatch at any moment, and when it does, you will be blasted to smithereens."

Marino gave her a sidelong look but eased away from her. "Where is the other White Eyes?" he demanded.

"He is seasick," Rock said, gesturing into the cabin.

Daisy's heart lurched as Marino swam past her into the cabin toward the mound of kelp.

"I wouldn't get too close!" Daisy warned. "Seasickness is highly contagious."

Marino lifted some tendrils of sea kelp, then started to sift rapidly through it, sending kelp swirling through the water. He swung around to Daisy. "Where is he?" he said.

Daisy thought fast. "He's vanished. I turned him into a pile of kelp. I'm a sea witch. And if you don't bring Maldew, I'll turn you into kelp, too."

But Marino was back to shuffling through the kelp. And it wasn't long before he got down to the hatch in the floor. He snatched it open and disappeared into the darkness below.

Moments later, he swam back out of the cabin, his face grim. "He escaped through a hole. The master is right. You are a liar!" Marino said.

Daisy said with mounting ferocity, "Yes, but I'm not lying when I say that this egg is about to hatch, and if Maldew isn't here when it does, he will not be its master. *I* will, and the first thing I will command it to do is destroy all the Red Eyes!"

The Red Eyes absorbed this information with blank faces before panic set in and they started to jabber among themselves.

"Quiet!" Marino shouted. "I can't think!" He hunched his shoulders in thought. After a bit, he said to the Red Eyes who had been guarding the egg, "You four take the White Eyes and the egg to the master. The rest of you, come with me."

"Where are we going, Marino?" Rock asked.

"After the White Eyes. When I find him, I will turn him."

"Turn him?" Daisy bleated.

"Red!" said Marino.

Daisy closed her eyes and prayed that Jesse and Coral were out of the Coral Jungle by now. In the meantime, she had no choice but to carry out her part of the plan and hope for the best.

With two Red Eyes behind her and two leading the way, Daisy set out for the Inner Circle.

When they got there, Emmy was still where she had been when Daisy last saw her, huddled in the ancient diving helmet. She lifted her head when she saw Daisy and waved a feeble fin.

"Just a little while longer," Daisy whispered to her, even though she doubted Emmy could hear through the iron and glass that imprisoned her and the junkyard of iron that surrounded her.

"Well, White Eyes," Maldew bubbled at her. "What news?"

"The news is good," Daisy said, lifting the soft-ball toward the Mermage's mouth.

"It has cracked!" Maldew said in excitement.

"That's why I had the Red Eyes bring me to you," Daisy said. "It could hatch anytime now."

"Where are the other White Eyes?" Maldew said.

One of the Red eyes started to say something but Daisy cut him off. "Don't worry about them," she told Maldew. "I'm the White Eyes you want for the job."

"Is there anything you need, White Eyes?" Maldew asked.

Daisy had no idea what to say to this. She was supposed to be an expert. On TV and in movies, people assisting in births always asked for hot water and strips of clean cloth. If there wasn't any cloth, they asked for newspapers, which Daisy had never really understood. But none of these items were available at the bottom of the sea, so she said, "We're good. All we can do is watch and wait and hope for a healthy hatchling."

"You had better hope," said Maldew in a menacing tone.

"I know, I know," Daisy said wearily. "Otherwise the consequences will be unspeakable."

Daisy made the egg hop around in her hand like a hot potato. "It's really beginning to heat up. I'd stand back if I were you. If it explodes, I can't be responsible for the damages. Oh, that's right, you can't stand back. You can't move. Well, then, I'll stand back. Whoopsie!"

Daisy deliberately opened her hands and let the egg drop. It fell slowly through the water and bounced back up from the seafloor. "Wow," she said, catching it one-handed. "This dragon egg's pretty bouncy. You'd think it was a ball or something."

Maldew bristled and the water around him boiled. "It *is* a ball. White Eyes, you have fooled me. WHERE IS THE REAL EGG? TELL ME BEFORE I STRANGLE YOU WITH SEA SNAKES!"

"I could have sworn this was the way out," Coral said to Jesse.

"I think we've been swimming in circles. I'm pretty sure we've passed that twist of coral before," Jesse said. "I remember thinking it looked like a charred pelican."

Coral bit her lip and looked around. "I don't get it. The widening spot that leads to the exit we always use is supposed to be right there." Where Coral pointed there was an impenetrable thicket of coral.

"Maybe the stuff moves around," Jesse offered.

"It never has before," Coral said.

"Is it me or is the whole jungle thicker than it was before?" Jesse said.

"Now that you mention it," Coral said, looking warily about her, "I am feeling kind of dizzy."

"Maldew did this thing earlier," Jesse said. "He sucked a bunch of iron out of the jungle. All sorts of things were blowing around. It was like this huge undersea hurricane. Maybe he rearranged the jungle when he did that."

"Maybe," Coral said.

"Also, we got him really mad," Jesse said. "Maybe when he gets really mad, the coral gets denser."

Coral nodded. "Okay, then maybe we should swim *up* instead of *out* of the jungle. This egg isn't getting any cooler."

They both looked down at the egg in the oven mitt. It was giving off a dull red glow.

"We'd better get moving," Jesse said.

But when they began the upward swim, they saw that the coral was every bit as dense above them as it was around them. Still, they had no choice but to begin weaving in and out of the coral, squeezing through the narrow places between branches. It wasn't long before Jesse's arms were covered with stinging welts.

When the six Red Eyes came crashing down upon them through the thicket, Coral was so startled she nearly dropped the egg.

"Watch it, dudes!" Coral yelled. "We've got a live egg here."

Marino said, "That is not the egg. The egg is back with the other White Eyes."

Jesse laughed uneasily. "That's what you think. That one was a fake. This is the real deal."

The egg flared up like a live coal and Marino pulled back, along with the other five Red Eyes.

Marino turned on Jesse. "The master will be furious. This is *your* doing!" he said.

"Well, that is true," Jesse said modestly. With one hand behind his back, he signaled to Coral to flee while he distracted the Red Eyes. "It *was* my idea, if I do say so myself. Where I come from, they call me the Man with the Plan."

All six Red Eyes with tridents gathered around Jesse, glaring.

"Hey, fellas, nice to see you again," Jesse said. "Really. I missed you. I'd be happy to tell you the story of the egg, if you'd care to listen. Far up in the northwestern territories, two dragons lived in a cave halfway up the side of a mountain—"

"No more listening to White Eyes," Marino said.

Jesse couldn't see past the wall of Red Eyes, but he hoped that Coral had made off with the egg. "Oh, come on, guys!" Jesse said. "Can't we please discuss this like civilized—"

"No more discussions with White Eyes," Marino growled. "White Eyes lie!"

"Yeah, well, what can I tell you? White Eyes tell white lies," Jesse babbled.

"It ends now," said Marino, reaching out to touch Jesse's arm, just as the other five also laid hands on him.

Chapter Twelve

SOUNDING THE BOATSWAIN'S PIPE

Jesse squeezed his eyes shut and waited to be turned into a Red Eyes. How would it feel when it happened? Would his brain suddenly turn to sludge? Would his muscles go limp or start to bulge like the

Red Eyes who were touching him? Would his eyes burn? But nothing like any of that happened.

He eased his eyes open, one at a time, and looked. The six Red Eyes dropped their hands and stared at them. The green tinge was draining from their fingers, their arms, their torsos, and their faces, and finally, the redness cleared from their eyes. They shook their heads, their braids swinging, as they turned and stared at each other in wonder.

"You're White Eyes!" Jesse said.

The mermen dropped their tridents, raised their hands above their heads, and bowed low to Jesse.

"Bodacious move, brody!" Coral darted out from behind a clump of coral.

"I thought you'd gotten away," Jesse said.

"I started to," said Coral, "but I couldn't leave you high and dry."

"I think it's more like low and wet," said Jesse. "But thanks anyway. I guess."

"O most powerful Mermage!" said Marino. "You are our master now!"

Jesse smiled. "No, I'm not," he said. "And I'm not a Mermage. It's the magical dragon ichor on my skin that saved you. Honest." Jesse held out his arms and showed the mermen the white spots where their fingers had touched him and the ichor had come off on them.

"We have been under the Mermage's power for so long," said Marino, his flat voice now carrying a lively lilt. "You have no idea what torture it is to serve a master you despise."

"Then why did you do it?" Jesse asked.

"The Mermage worms his way into our brains. He makes us do his bidding. Do you think Rock and I *wanted* to steal on board *The Golden Dragon* and take the egg? But Maldew put the thought into our heads until we had no choice but to obey his will. Now we are our own selves again, thanks to you, and we are forever in your debt," said Marino. "What can we do to repay you?"

Jesse and Coral exchanged a look, their faces lighting up. They knew just the thing!

Back in the Inner Circle, Daisy was trying to keep calm in the face of the Mermage's rage. "The real Thunder Egg is back on board *The Golden Dragon,* safe and sound, and about to hatch," she informed him.

"You stand there and tell me this and expect me to let you live another moment of your paltry White-Eyed existence?" Maldew said in a rumbling burble.

"I do," said Daisy. "You see, I had this big fight with the other two White Eyes. They wanted to escape and take the egg back to the ship. But I wanted to stay and save my dragon, Emerald. The fact is, I want to save her so badly that I am willing to trade you the hatchling for Emerald."

"Tell me more and be quick about it, White Eyes," the Mermage burbled.

"If you let Emerald go," Daisy said, doling out her words with care, "I will take you to where the egg is about to hatch. If you witness the hatching, you will become the dragon's Keeper."

"How do you know this, White Eyes?" he asked.

"Because I'm not really a dragon doula. What I really am is a Dragon *Keeper*. And I know exactly how it works. Whosoever is in the presence of the hatchling at birth will be its Keeper. The dragon then lives to serve its Keeper. This dragon you see before you is mine. I am her Keeper. But I'm not greedy. I don't need two dragons. You take the unborn one. I'll take Emerald. And we'll call it even."

Daisy crossed her fingers as she watched the giant sea slug simmer and seethe. Finally, Maldew said, "That's all very well, White Eyes, but how do I get to the egg? For all my power, I cannot move."

"No problem. Emerald is a very powerful dragon. Free her from that iron helmet and I will command her to move you to where the egg is. I swear, on the head of my own beautiful dragon, that I will do this," she said.

"The dragon serves you, White Eyes? Only think of how well a dragon would serve *me*!" the Mermage mused to himself. "No more feeble-minded Red Eyes at my beck and call. I will have my own personal dragon!" As if fueled by thoughts of all he would do, the Mermage began to puff up.

As the others had done before, the Red Eyes lifted their tridents and plunged them into the sand. They all watched as Maldew expanded to a blimp-sized blowfish again. When it seemed he could get no bigger, with a loud *blat,* he released a torrent of bubbles.

Suddenly, the water was filled with flying metal objects—spearguns and pilings and chains. The Red Eyes hung on fast to their tridents, their tails whipping behind them like wind socks in a high gale. Daisy was blown backward, tumbling head over tail, toward the edge of the clearing. If it hadn't been for the anchor flipping past her—which she grabbed hold of and which in turn, dug into the ocean floor—she would have been blown clean back into a stinging patch of black coral.

When the bubbles and the debris finally subsided, the pieces of iron had all been blown clear of

Maldew's vicinity, including the diving helmet.

There was Emmy, still a dragon fish but a *free* dragon fish. The color came rushing back to her pallid scales. When she reached full ruddiness, she transformed back into a big green dragon.

The Red Eyes gasped and cowered.

"Nicely done, Mally-dew-*doo*!" Emmy said saucily.

"Welcome back, Emmy," said Daisy, letting go of the anchor and swimming to her. "Have you been following what's been going on?" she asked.

"I read lips," said Emmy. "Even his ultra-supersonic gross ones."

"Well, then," said Daisy, "let's get Maldew to *The Golden Dragon* in time to witness the hatching. That's the deal."

Emmy pulled herself up tall. "Not when you're dealing with a fat, evil slug it isn't," Emmy said with an ornery look in her eye. "I'm not letting this monster anywhere near my baby sibling. I'd sooner get stuck back in that diving helmet for all eternity."

"White Eyes!" Maldew thundered. "Control your impudent dragon!"

"I'm not impudent," Emmy said haughtily. "For your information, like the lady said, I have *gumption*."

"Emmy," Daisy said, swimming still closer and

meeting Emmy's stubborn look with a stern one of her own. "Who's the Keeper here? You or me?"

Emmy hung her head. "You are, Daisy Flower," she said.

"Then you're just going to have to trust your Keeper that she has everybody's—and I mean *everybody's*—best interests at heart, and go along with *the plan*," said Daisy.

"There's a plan?" Emmy snapped out of her sulk.

"Always," Daisy said.

Emmy nodded slowly, understanding kindling in her eyes. "Aye, aye," she said, snapping off a smart salute. "Chief Cargo Mate, Emerald of Leandra, reporting for duty. I understand you have a big load that needs transporting, Captain Daisy?"

"The biggest," Daisy said with a wide grin. "And fast."

"Hmm," said Emmy, frowning in thought as she swam around Maldew's enormous bulk several times. Then she stopped on the long side and hunkered down. Her irises began to spin like a set of brilliant green pinwheels. Her nostrils gave off three peppery pinkish bubbles, which rose up and radiated outward, filling the clearing in the Coral Jungle with a bright, hot, pulsating light.

When the light cleared, Daisy expected to see

that Maldew's massive bulk had moved. But Maldew was right where he had always been, since the time his ooze had first settled into the body of the sea cucumber that fateful day.

"What happened?" Daisy asked Emmy.

"Zero, zilch, nada, zippo," Emmy said with a perplexed sigh. "Nothing at all happened."

"You call that dragon magic, White Eyes?" Maldew rumbled scornfully.

"Shut up, Bait Breath," Emmy said, waving a distracted paw at him. "Let a dragon ponder the problem."

"Maybe being trapped in iron dampened your powers?" Daisy said. "Maybe if you rest up a bit, your powers will return."

"Nope," said Emmy, shaking her head firmly. "That won't do any good at all. My powers are up to speed. It's Belleweather. She's *good*. The spell she put on Maldew is locked in. I can't unlock it. I'm afraid we're just going to have to move him the old-fashioned way."

"You mean carry him?" Daisy asked.

Emmy's look turned sly. "I mean drag him."

"*Drag* him?" Daisy echoed.

"Well, I'm a *dra*gon, aren't I? Who drags better than a dragon, I ask you?" Emmy said.

Daisy frowned.

"Buck up, Daisy Flower," Emmy said. "All we need is a big old sturdy fishing net." She turned to the Red Eyes. "Don't just stand there with your muscles bulging. Go find me a fish net big enough to hold your master and make it snappy. We've got a date with a dragon egg."

The squad of Red Eyes swam off into the jungle and returned in no time with a fishing net that was twice as big as Maldew.

"Good work, dudes," Emmy said. "Now grab the net along the edges and, at my signal, you're going to swim this sucker under the bulk of your boss. When I lift him, you swim it under him. Got it? Ready? One, two, three, lift!"

With a series of mighty grunts, Emmy lifted just enough of Maldew's gristly bulk for the two columns of Red Eyes to swim underneath the length of the sea cucumber, spreading the net beneath him. When they made it to the other end, Emmy dropped the last bit of Maldew on top of the net.

"Watch it, Dragon," Maldew growled.

"Watch yourself," Emmy said. "I'm sacrificing my baby sibling to you. But nobody ever said I had to like it. Okay now." She swung around to the Red Eyes. "I want you to round up all the Red Eyes in the jungle and bring them back here. It's going to take all of us pulling together to move him all the way to *The Golden Dragon*."

The Red Eyes again swam off. Almost immediately, they began to gather in the clearing: more Red Eyes than Daisy had ever seen at one time, in one place. It was creepy but it was also a little awesome. Like an army of Egyptian slaves banding together to drag one of those giant blocks that built the great pyramids. The Red Eyes formed a circle around the sea slug, each one holding a part of the fishing net.

"We'll move him headfirst," Emmy said, taking up a position at the net by the Mermage's bubbling mouth.

The Mermage said, "White Eyes, this will never work."

Daisy, who hovered off to the side, watched as the mob of Red Eyes, led by Emmy, started to drag the net holding Maldew across the seafloor. She gnawed on her lower lip. Maldew might be right. They moved inch by inch. At the rate they were going, it would take forever. By the time they got to *The Golden Dragon,* the baby would not only be hatched, but it would also be as big as a sea cow.

As Daisy fidgeted with the seashell on the fishing line around her neck, her hand grazed the chain of the boatswain's pipe. She had forgotten that Jesse had given it to her. Then the thought occurred to her: They were beset by perils, weren't they? Or, at the very least, they needed help.

She put the pipe to her lips and blew on it with all her might. No sound came out. Nothing happened. Not even the faintest suggestion of bubbles.

Elsewhere in the Coral Jungle at that very moment, Rock and four other newly transformed White Eyes accompanied Coral and the egg, leaving Marino behind with Jesse.

"I hope they make it to the beach before the egg hatches," Jesse said, staring after them.

"They'll make it," Marino said.

"But the Coral Jungle seems to be getting thicker," Jesse said gloomily.

"The tridents will help," said Marino. "See?"

Jesse watched as the five mermen, swimming ahead of Coral, waved the tridents at the black coral. Wherever the tridents touched, the black coral turned into seaweed that drifted, like brightly colored tissue paper, harmlessly out of their way.

"How did they do that?" Jesse asked Marino.

Marino held up his own trident. "These are forged from Maldew's original trident. While we were under Maldew's power, they did only his bidding. But now that we are free, they will have to obey us."

"Can your trident help me double-time it to *The Golden Dragon*?" Jesse asked. Then he quickly shared with Marino the details of the plan.

As Marino listened to Jesse, his smile grew ever wider until he positively beamed. "What a grand plan!" he said. "I will be happy to take part in it, along with my trident."

Marino turned the trident around so that the tines were facing away from them. With one hand, Marino held on to the handle near the top, placing Jesse's hand below his, just as the trident's three iron tines fired up like the engine of a small jet rocket. The next thing Jesse knew, they were hurtling through the jungle, the black coral bursting like fireworks into bright seaweed all around them.

"Rock?" said Daisy. She barely recognized the merman who swam up to her, with his white skin and clear eyes. "What happened to you?"

"Dragon ichor turned me into a White Eyes. All six of us. It happened when we laid hands on Jesse to turn him," Rock said. "He turned *us* instead."

"That's great," Daisy said. "Does that mean Jesse made it back to *The Golden Dragon*?"

"Marino is taking him there now," Rock said.

"We escorted Coral and the egg safely to the beach. Please," he said, nodding toward the mob of Red Eyes who were dragging the net, "touch them and turn them to White Eyes. Let them suffer no longer."

"I wish I could," Daisy said. "But first I have to swim up through the coral to the surface and blow on this pipe. It doesn't seem to work underwater, and we need help moving your former master to the ship."

"I can get you there very quickly," said Rock. "Hold on to my trident."

One minute Daisy was wrapping her fingers around the handle of Rock's trident. The next minute, she was shooting upward through a colorful tunnel of swirling seaweed that grew brighter the closer to the surface they came. Then the seaweed faded away as the water lightened to pale aquamarine shot through with sunlight.

Daisy hadn't realized until that moment how badly she had missed the sun until it beamed down upon her face through the water. It was morning sun, warm and golden. The next moment, her head broke the surface of the water. She let go of the trident and drank in the fresh air.

Rock floated next to her, smiling, his face lifted toward the sun. Daisy noticed immediately that she was only about a half mile from the beach in front of the Inn of the Barking Seal and that the seals were, as always, barking. She never thought she would be so happy to hear that sound.

Daisy fastened her lips around the gun of the boatswain's pipe. Closing and opening her hand over the hole in the sphere, she sent out one long, low burst and two short, high ones. This time the pipe sounded, loud and clear.

Chapter Thirteen

THE SACRED DRACONIAN BIRTHING INCANTATION

The seals fell instantly silent. The next moment, Daisy heard a loud splashing sound as the seals slipped off the rock and into the sea, one after another until the big flat rock was empty.

The seals were swimming swiftly toward her.

Daisy ducked back beneath the sea. Soon, the water around her and Rock was swarming with the sinuous black and gray bodies of seals. There must have been hundreds of them, brushing against her, their golden eyes filled with alert intelligence, their whiskery noses pointed toward her, awaiting further instructions.

"Follow us!" she cried as she headed back down into the jungle.

Rock led the way, his trident turning any black coral it touched into harmless puffs and swirls of seaweed.

When Emmy saw Daisy at the head of the massive club of seals, she dropped the net and cried out, "You brought help! Good work, Daisy!"

"I blew the boatswain's pipe and look what came a-swimmin'!" Daisy called out.

Without even being told what to do, the seals took up places along the net, doubling the workforce. With the seals' assistance, the net holding Maldew now skimmed across the seafloor as fast as a nuclear sub on an urgent mission. Daisy had to whip her tail like mad to keep up with them. It wasn't long before the big orange fan coral flashed past. When the jawbone of the Leviathan loomed ahead, Daisy knew that their final destination was near.

Daisy swam up abreast of Emmy and said, "Take the cargo around to the stern." She shifted her eyes to Maldew. "I believe you'll find the 'dragon egg' in the captain's cabin."

Emmy winked. "Aye, aye, Skipper," she said as she and the crew tugged Maldew sternward.

Soon, they arrived at the high windows of the captain's cabin, which was flanked by portholes. Inside, the cabin glowed cozily with the light of a dozen phosphairy lanterns.

Daisy swam up to a window and peered inside. There was Jesse standing over the chart table. As planned, he had obtained a prop from the Armory. The Revolutionary War solid-shot cannonball was encrusted with white barnacles. From this distance, it was a dead ringer for a Thunder Egg. It lay in the center of their backpack.

Yar stood by the counter between the brass telescope and the crystal ball. Fluke hovered midway between Yar and Jesse. When Jesse looked up at the windows and saw them, he began to wave his hands over the egg, his lips moving feverishly, muttering mumbo jumbo.

Daisy turned and signaled Emmy to bring the

load closer. The host of bearers dragged the net so that Maldew's nose was pressed up against the porthole glass.

"What's the White Eyes doing?" the Mermage demanded.

"He's uttering the Ultra-Supersonic-Sacred Draconian Birthing Incantation," Daisy said.

"But I can't hear him! I want to hear every word that's being uttered," the Mermage whined.

"That can be arranged," said Emmy. She bashed the porthole and picked away the shards of glass. Then she gave Maldew one last good shove so that his business end bulged through the porthole into the cabin. "There you go, Super Cuke. You've got a ringside seat."

Emmy would never be able to squeeze him all the way into the cabin. He would never fit. But they had agreed that so long as *part of him* was inside the cabin, their plan might just stand a chance of working.

Jesse stopped moving his lips. He looked up. First he winked at Daisy. Then he said to the Mermage, "Welcome aboard, Maldew. We thought you'd never get here."

Jesse directed a solemn nod at Fluke.

Fluke nodded at Yar. "Give it a bit of a twist, will you, Chief?" she said.

"A twist, you say, Cap'n?" Yar asked.

"Yes, like the time you wrenched open that tasty jar of grapefruit marmalade left over from the *Titanic*. Remember, Chief?" Fluke said.

"Dashed delectable stuff it was, too. Twisting, Cap'n." Yar turned from the telescope and wrapped his finny hands around the coral base of the crystal ball. With a grunt and a snort, he gave it a good vigorous wrenching.

A mighty roaring sound rose up through the hull, like thousands of tons of water pounding down, like Niagara Falls going over the rocky shelf and thundering into the gorge below.

When the roaring stopped, Daisy uncovered her eyes. Jesse, Fluke, and Yar had disappeared from the cabin. But, more importantly, Maldew was also gone.

Daisy squeezed through the porthole and swam over to gaze into the crystal ball. There was Maldew's great green, red-bristled bulk, laid out on the beach in front of the Driftwoods' shack.

"Yes!" she said.

A sea cucumber, no matter how big, Jesse had assured them all when he had proposed his plan, could not survive very long on dry land.

Just then, Daisy heard a great commotion coming from above deck. She swam to the porthole just in time to see hundreds of sprites, kelpies, selkies, merfolk, and a vast assortment of undersea creatures, from penguins to polar bears, come tumbling down from the ship to join the Red Eyes and the seals.

But something was happening to the Red Eyes. They looked around at each other in wonder as the green tinge drained from their skin, their bloodshot eyes cleared, and their fingernails turned pale and pearly. The rest of the Red Eyes had become White Eyes.

The passengers of *The Golden Dragon* pumped the hands of the newly transformed White Eyes and clapped them heartily on their backs. Then everyone froze as a sound like a very loud foghorn filled the water. When they started moving again, it was as one body, pouring through the white arch and disappearing from sight.

Star swam up to the porthole. "Are you coming?" she asked.

"Where's everyone going?" Daisy asked.

"To the hatching," Star said happily. "Follow me."

"Oh!" said Daisy. She had been so intent on carrying out their plan, she had almost forgotten the reason for it in the first place: the Thunder Egg.

Daisy squeezed herself back out of the porthole and followed Star through the arch.

On the beach, Maldew's body was already beginning to dry in the rays of the midmorning sun.

Jesse was in too much discomfort to appreciate the moment of victory. He couldn't breathe. His tail flopped helplessly in the sand. Just when a great blackness began closing in on him, Mitzi knelt beside him and laid her cool hands on either side of his face. Her shiny dark eyes looked deeply into his. His tail stopped flopping and his legs and feet, in their jeans and sneakers, kicked their way out of their sheath of scales.

He lay back in the sand and took a long, shaky breath of air, his first in days. His hands dug into the dry sand, reveling in the dry, gritty feel of it. Then he reached up and groped behind his ears just as the last of his six gills sealed shut beneath his sandy fingers. The dragon ichor, he noticed, had also disappeared from his hands and arms.

"Thanks, Captain Belleweather," he said as he sat up.

"Call me Mitzi. And it's my thanks that go out to all of you," she said. "You saved the life of a precious dragon, and you've rid the Eighth Sea of the greatest scourge it has ever known."

Jesse looked around and his eyes fell on Fluke and Yar. They were flopping around in the sand, gasping and wheezing.

"Please help them!" Jesse pleaded. He knew exactly how they felt.

But Emmy beat Mitzi to it. She bent over and picked one of them up in each arm. Gently, she carried them down to the water's edge and set them loose in the surf. They dived beneath the waves and their heads bobbed up beyond the line of the breaking surf.

"Thank you, Emerald!" Fluke called out.

"Good show, what?" said Yar. "Say, who's got the egg now?"

"We've got the egg!" Emmy and Reef called out to them, pumping fists in the air.

"Jolly good show!" Yar said with a wave of his finny hand. "Pity, though, after all this, we'll miss the hatching."

"No, you won't," said Mitzi. "Swim through the Arch of Leviathan and we'll meet you in the Back Bay. We're holding the hatching in there. It's too unpleasant here on the beach," she said, indicating the festering body of Maldew.

"Ra*ther*," said Yar.

"Quite!" said Fluke.

Then the selkie and the kelpie dipped beneath the waves.

The sea cucumber seemed to be rapidly shrinking in the sun. But the smaller it got, the more disgusting it smelled. Only the seagulls seemed able to tolerate it. In fact, it was as if they had found a delicacy. They wheeled overhead, diving and plucking off little bits of green slime and red gristle, then flying off with it.

Jesse was glad Daisy wasn't here. Although scavenging was a perfectly natural process, he knew she would find the spectacle of the seabirds picking over the carrion truly gross. Then he realized that if Daisy wasn't here, she would miss the hatching.

"Somebody needs to find Daisy!" he called out.

"Dude. Maintain your mellow." Bill Driftwood leaned over him and held out a hand.

At first, Jesse thought he was going to do the handshake, but then he realized he was just offering Jesse a hand up. "Come on into the sugar shack," said Bill. "I'll bet my Marc Newson nickel-plated elephant-gun surfboard that your cousin's already waiting for you in the Back Bay with Corey. They're tending the egg. Last time I looked in, it was shaking, rattling, and rolling, so it must be time."

"Corey?" Jesse asked. He was still in a bit of a

daze and he felt more than a little wobbly on his feet.

"That's what we call Coral," Bill said, catching Jesse's elbow as he stumbled. "It might take you a while to get your lubber legs back."

Jesse, Bill, and Emmy followed Reef and Mitzi as they skirted the corpse of the sea cucumber and headed toward the small ramshackle structure, made of driftwood and sea salvage, set into the side of the cliff. The front door hung on a set of rusty hinges that protested loudly when Bill Driftwood hauled it open.

"Groovy guests go first," he said with a gallant sweep of his sun-bronzed arm.

Emmy squeezed through the tiny door first with catlike agility. "Jesse Tiger," she said from the other side, "you are going to dig these digs."

Jesse stepped into the shack, holding his breath. Having already been on board the magical square-rigger, Jesse figured he was in for a real treat. But nothing he imagined could have prepared him for this.

He let out his breath in a long gasp of astonishment. A vast astrodome made of sea glass and coral, sparkling in the sunlight, rose up around him. High up near the ceiling, he saw the suggestion of other smaller, cozier rooms accessible by a series of rope ladders. There were ropes to swing from and even trapezes. It would be like living in a giant, magical, seaside circus tent.

"I want a tour," said Jesse, barely able to contain his excitement.

Emmy cleared her throat loudly.

Reef grinned. "Yeah, well, there's a kinda, sorta more important matter we need to tend to first, don't ya think?" he said.

Jesse blushed. "The egg!" How could he have forgotten the egg?

Reef clapped him on the back. "Chill out, dude. Seeing this house for the first time can rattle your rigging. But after the hatching, *if* I can get away, I'll be happy to show you around. I've got an awesome computer setup in my room. And Daisy's going to groove to the max on Corey's seashell collection."

"That 'his' and 'hers' cabin we stayed in on the *Dragon* was yours and Coral's, wasn't it?" Jesse asked.

"Yeah, Mom made it for us years before we were even born, but Corey and I haven't actually seen it ourselves yet," Reef said. "Maldew's curse kept my mom out of the Eighth. But now that he's gone, the curse is lifted and she can go back."

"This way, dudes," Emmy said, following Bill and Mitzi Driftwood down a long hallway that was lined with brightly painted surfboards—long boards, short boards, wood and fiberglass, wildly painted with sharks and orchids and bolts of lightning.

"They're in the Back Bay," Reef explained. "We decided to have the hatching there so all our cousins from the Eighth could catch it. It's gonna be a totally bodacious happening."

It was like stepping inside a giant geode. The Back Bay was a big pool of azure water whose reflection shimmered and danced on the walls of a blue crystal grotto. The pool was teeming with selkies and kelpies and sea sprites and merfolk and phosphairies and all manner of undersea creatures. Jesse saw Star and Fluke and Yar among them, as well as Marino and Rock with all the other exguards of the Mermage. From the waist up, they looked like a team of lifeguards.

Yar, hailing Jesse, opened his mouth to say something but then seemed to think better of it and merely shook his head and pointed with his finny hand toward Coral and Daisy.

At first, Jesse didn't recognize Daisy without her tail. The two girls, both dressed in jeans and sneakers and sweatshirts, were hunkered down on the shore of the pool with the backpack stretched out on the ground between them. On top of the backpack, the egg rocked quickly back and forth.

Except for the gentle lapping of the water against the shore, it was very nearly silent in the Back Bay, unless you knew what to listen for, and Jesse knew. It was a *creak-creak* sound, like the door to a magical realm being opened ever so slowly.

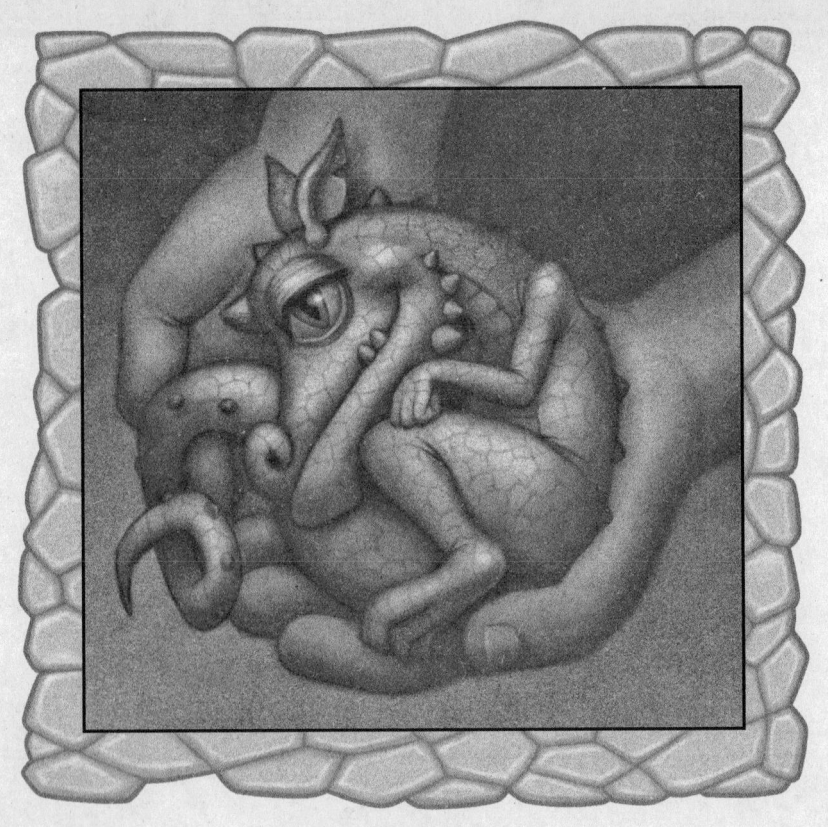

Chapter Fourteen

GOLDEN OF LEANDRA

Jesse and Emmy, followed by the Driftwoods, hurried to join Coral and Daisy by the pool of the Back Bay. When Daisy saw them approach, she rose to her feet, stepped away from the egg, and let Reef take her place.

202

That was the moment when Jesse understood who the lucky Keepers of this hatching dragon were going to be: Coral and Reef.

Daisy took Jesse's hand and squeezed hard. "It's happening, Jess!" she whispered. "Our second hatching."

"Their first one," Jesse whispered back, nodding toward Coral and Reef.

Reef looked up at his parents, who stood next to Emmy, an unspoken question in his eyes. Mitzi nodded slowly and smiled her encouragement. Reef knelt next to Coral, who picked up the egg and held it in one hand. Reef joined his hand with hers, and together they cupped the Thunder Egg in a nest made of hands. Either the egg had cooled down some, Jesse figured, or the Driftwood kids had hands like catchers' mitts.

All of a sudden, the egg stopped rocking. Then it started to vibrate, giving off a high-pitched sound, like a tuning fork. The sound grew louder and louder, then fainter, before falling silent. Then— just like that!—the Thunder Egg cracked open, exactly down the middle.

Carefully, Coral picked the two pieces of the geode away with her free hand. The geode had golden crystals inside.

Bill nudged Jesse and Daisy. Hesitantly, they

joined Reef and Coral. Coral handed one half each to Jesse and Daisy. But the cousins weren't paying much attention to the geode. The baby dragon was all they saw.

The tiny dragon sitting in those cupped hands was the same golden color as the crystals of the egg that had held it for over a hundred years. Its eyes were huge and luminous and golden. Everyone in the Back Bay watched for a few moments in hushed silence, marveling at the creature's miniature perfection.

"It's a boy!" Emmy said, breaking the silence. "Everybody, please welcome Golden of Leandra! Son of Leandra and Obsidian. And Brother of Emerald."

"Emmy-world!" said the tiny creature, cocking his little head at the big green dragon looming over him. Then he turned to look at Reef.

"Weef!" said the tiny dragon, holding out his arms.

"That's right, little dude," said Reef.

Next, he turned to Coral. "Cowal!"

"Awwww. His little voice is so cute!" said Coral.

"Foooooood!" said Golden.

"I wonder what we should feed him," Reef said, looking to Jesse and Daisy.

Jesse and Daisy held up their hands.

"I'm pretty sure you'll have to solve that mystery for yourselves," said Daisy with a grin.

"Good luck," said Jesse. "You're going to love being Dragon Keepers."

"I think this calls for a sea tea party, what?" said Yar to Fluke.

"I couldn't agree more," said Fluke.

"And you don't feel too badly giving up the helm, do you?" Yar said.

"Not at all, Yar, dear," said Fluke. "The helm has always belonged to Captain Belleweather. I've merely been holding it for her."

"Thank you, Fluke," said Mitzi.

"Topping, what?" said Yar, looking around. "I say, where did that girl go? Star! Where is she? Doesn't she know it's sea teatime!"

"Here I am, sir!" Star popped up out of the water, hoisting a giant seashell tray with dozens of teacups. With her usual pert efficiency, she began to pass out cups to the guests.

"Star?" Rock said.

With the cups rattling on her tray, Star slowly turned and looked at Rock.

"Rocky?" she said in a trembling voice. "You're okay!"

"I'm more than okay, now that I see my little mermaid friend again," said Rock.

A selkie relieved Star of the tray. She lunged and threw herself into Rock's arms.

More full trays appeared after that, borne by sprites. Soon, there were hundreds of cups being passed around, from a thousand different tea sets filled with a vast variety of seaweeds.

"Oh, excellent!" said Yar. "We have dulce here, fresh from the Arctic currents. And *Laminaria japonica* from the pristine waters off Japan. We have Wakame and laver and Ma-kombu, too! We've got everything we need when it comes to seaweed. Oh, sea tea *does* bring out the poet in me!"

"Don't I know it, dear?" said Fluke fondly.

"Do you have any sea tea from the Sargasso Sea?" Jesse asked. "We really liked that stuff, didn't we, Emmy? Emmy?"

He looked around. Emmy wasn't there. "Hey! Has anyone seen our dragon?" Jesse called out.

"She must have slipped out when no one was looking," said Mitzi.

Jesse and Daisy left everyone to watch the new-born dragon toddling along the banks of the pool. They ran back down the long hallway lined with surfboards and burst out the front door of the shack.

The giant sea cucumber was now no more than a long green stain on the sand. Emmy stood in the shallow surf, staring out to sea.

"There you are!" said Daisy as she and Jesse went running to join her.

"Why did you leave so suddenly?" Jesse asked.

Emmy sighed shakily. "Go on, say it," she said.

"Say what?" Jesse said. "And would you mind coming up on the beach? I don't want to get my sneakers wet."

When he realized what he had just said, he shook his head and laughed at himself. But the expression on their dragon's face was no laughing matter. So he and Daisy waded into the surf, sneakers and all.

"Tell us what's bothering you, Emmy," Daisy said gently.

"Golden is sooooo beautiful," said Emmy.

"Yeah, he is," Jesse said slowly.

"And his Keepers are going to have such a gnarly time of it with their baby dragon," Emmy said.

"True," said Jesse. "Just like we had a gnarly time of it with you. And we're having a hyperfierce gnar-gnar time now that you're all grown . . . well, almost all grown . . . at least, we hope nearly all grown," he added lamely, looking up at her.

Emmy turned to gaze down at him, her eyes brightening. "You really mean that? Hyperfierce?"

"Ultra-supersonic hyperfierce gnar-gnar," said

Jesse. "The bigger you get, the gnarlier our adventures become."

"You're sure?" said Emmy. She gathered the two of them up in her arms. "You're the best Keepers a dragon ever had."

"Next to Reef and Coral," Daisy said.

"Next to Reef and Coral," said Emmy. "I know my baby brother is in the grooviest of good hands."

"Far out!" Jesse and Daisy said as Emmy set them down on the dry sand.

Just then, they heard the sound of a foghorn blowing, followed by a giant *whoosh*. They looked out to sea, and there, riding the waves just beyond the big rocks, was *The Golden Dragon,* sails unfurled and dripping, in all her square-rigged splendor.

Mitzi and Bill, followed by Coral and Reef, came piling out the door of the shack. Reef carried Golden. Jesse noticed that he was wearing the oven mitt to protect his hand from Golden's needle-sharp talons, just as Jesse had once worn a purple kneesock. Coral carried the backpack by one strap.

"You'll be wanting your backpack back," said Coral, handing it to Jesse.

"Thanks," said Jesse. He and Daisy took the two halves of the golden geode and tucked them into the side pouch. "These'll make a great addition to our Museum of Magic," he said as he zipped up the pouch and slipped his arms through the straps.

"All right, lubbers," said Captain Mitzi Belleweather-Driftwood. "It's time for us to take our water dragon and set sail. The best place to rear a water dragon is at sea."

Jesse's shoulders sagged. "But I never got my tour of the sugar shack."

"Next time," Reef promised.

"Does that mean we'll be seeing you again?" Daisy asked.

"Of course we will, silly," said Emmy. "No one, not even her Keepers, can keep me away from my baby brother."

"Chillax, dude. The sand witches will let us know the next time you visit Polly," said Bill. "And we'll drop anchor so you dudes and dudettes can visit us on board. *And* tour the sugar shack."

"Solid," Jesse said, and he did the super surfer handshake, first with Bill and then with Coral, the fist-bump, wiggety-waggety, chest-thump, slap-slap-snap routine that Jesse had been practicing in his mind since he was first introduced to it by Surfer Bill, the husband of Captain Mitzi, the Selkie Enchantress. He would have gone on to do the handshake with Reef, too, but Reef's hands were otherwise occupied. And Jesse didn't feel right doing anything but giving Captain Belleweather a crisp salute.

"Come on, Keepers," said Emmy. "I'll fly you two back to the Inn of the Barking Seal. What do you want to bet Polly saved you some turkey?"

Jesse didn't know how to tell Emmy that there was no way there would be enough cold turkey for her, too.

Emmy read his mind. "Chillax, little dude. No turkey for me. I have a date to dine on sushi at my club tonight."

"Your club?" Jesse and Daisy chimed.

"Yeah, my seal club. Ever heard of seals? Those whiskery little critters that lie on the big rock and say *arf-arf-arf* all night and day? I'm going to try and see if I can get a word in edgewise."

"Do us a favor, Em, and find out why they do that *arf*ing business all the time," Daisy said.

"Aye, aye, skippers," Emmy said, popping her wings. "Now, hop on board and it's over the river and through the woods to Grandmother's house we go." She sighed and chuckled. "You have no idea how much I've been looking forward to saying that."

Later that afternoon, Jesse sat at his grandmother's ancient computer and pounded out a belated Thanksgiving greeting to his parents.

Dear Mom and Dad,
How was Thanksgiving in Tanzania? What
did you guys have for turkey this year?
Remember the time we had roast bustard?
That was BAD news. We had a blast here
even though we lost the backpack for a
couple of days. But we got it back and we
also found a geode. Won't Uncle Joe be
surprised? Polly has new neighbors, Bill and
Mitzi Driftwood and their kids, Coral and
Reef. A bunch of hippie beach bums. Polly
says those are the best kind. Polly just
set down a turkey sandwich with sausage
stuffing and tons of mayonnaise. This is my
third sandwich. The first one came with a pile
of cucumber-dill salad, but Daisy and I both
said, "Hold the cucumbers, please!" I may
never be able to look at a cucumber again.
Like Daisy says, they are malankey. Want
to know how come that is? It's a looong
story . . . or should I say a thumping good
yarn. We just finished spinning it for Polly.
Maybe we'll spin it for you one of these days.
In the meantime, I am, as always, your loving
son in America,
Jesse Tiger

KATE KLIMO, daughter of a merchant sea captain, grew up in the little town of Sea Cliff, on Long Island's North Shore. Her best friend, Justine, lived in a house right across the street from the best swimming beach. Kate and Justine grew up "half-fish," spending their summer days searching for sea glass and buried pirate treasure and pretending to be mermaids. Now Kate lives in upstate New York, not far from a babbling brook, which flows to a stream that feeds into the Hudson River, which, in turn, flows to the Atlantic Ocean. Landlocked though she now may be, she visits the shore whenever she can and still believes that there is nothing on earth quite as magical as the sea.

Visit Kate's website, thedragonkeepers.com.

Christmas morning, Jesse woke up to Daisy's finger drilling a hole in his shoulder.

"What?" he muttered groggily. He felt a sudden cold draft on the side of his face.

"Look, Jess!" Daisy said, pointing out the window next to his bed.

Jesse turned and gaped in astonishment.

It was as if someone had come along during the night and smothered the world in whipped cream. Freshly fallen snow covered the ground and the rooftops, weighing down the bushes and tree branches. More snow fell from the sky, which was a soft, pale gray, unlike any sky Jesse had ever seen before.

Daisy flapped her hands. "I can't wait to see how Emmy likes her first snow!"

Ten minutes later, in boots and scarves and mittens and winter coats, Jesse and Daisy stepped outside.

"Race you to the Dell!" Daisy said. She leapt off the porch and immediately fell face-first into the snow. She sat up, spitting out snow and laughing. Jesse dived in after her. Picking up their feet, they giant-stepped through the thigh-high drifts. When they got to the laurel bushes, they slid through the tunnel on their bottoms and struggled to their feet on the other side.

The Dell lay before them, a vast white china bowl with a fine black crack in it where the brook cut through the snow. To the west, Old Mother Mountain rose up like a huge white ghost, mini avalanches tumbling down her steep shoulders. Every branch of every tree in the Deep Woods was coated with snow.

In contrast to all the whiteness, the old dairy barn stood out as if a fresh coat of red paint had been applied to it overnight. The snow banked up against the sides of the barn, pure and undisturbed. Strangely, Emmy hadn't set foot in it yet.

Jesse and Daisy went slipping and sliding down the hill. When they came to the front of the barn, they stopped short.

"Maybe she was up late," said Daisy.

"Maybe she doesn't even know it snowed," Jesse said.

"Wait till she sees!" said Daisy.

But the moment they slid the barn door open, they knew something was wrong. The warmth of Emmy's body normally kept the barn toasty, but this morning the barn was cold. They ran to the corn-crib. It was empty. They climbed up to the loft. Also empty.

Their dragon, Emerald of Leandra, was gone.

When they got back down the ladder, they saw

one of the sheets of paper they'd given Emmy the night before spread out on the planks of the Museum of Magic. It was anchored in place by the raw emerald. On her brand-new personal stationery, Emmy had written in her large loopy hand: "Dear J and D, Gone to help Santa. E of L." She had added her two-fanged smiley face.

"'Gone to help Santa'?" Daisy said. "What could that possibly mean?"

"I don't know," Jesse said, bewildered. "But we have to find out!"